The Last of the OGs 3

Tranay Adams

Lock Down Publications and Ca$h
Presents
The Last of the OGs 3
A Novel by *Tranay Adams*

The Last of the OGs 3

Lock Down Publications
P.O. Box 944
Stockbridge, Ga 30281
www.lockdownpublications.com

Lock Down Publications
Like our page on Facebook: Lock Down Publications @
www.facebook.com/lockdownpublications.ldp

Book interior design by: **Shawn Walker**
Edited by: **Tamira Butler**

Stay Connected with Us!

Text **LOCKDOWN** to 22828 to stay up-to-date with new releases, sneak peaks, contests and more…
Thank you!

Submission Guideline.

Submit the first three chapters of your completed manuscript to ldpsubmissions@gmail.com, subject line: Your book's title. The manuscript must be in a .doc file and sent as an attachment. Document should be in Times New Roman, double spaced and in size 12 font. Also, provide your synopsis and full contact information. If sending multiple submissions, they must each be in a separate email.

Have a story but no way to send it electronically? You can still submit to LDP/Ca$h Presents. Send in the first three chapters, written or typed, of your completed manuscript to:

LDP: Submissions Dept
P.O. Box 944
Stockbridge, Ga 30281

DO NOT send original manuscript. Must be a duplicate.

Provide your synopsis and a cover letter containing your full contact information.

Thanks for considering LDP and Ca$h Presents.

Let Me Holla At Chu!

Niggaz can call themselves the best all they want. It doesn't mean Jimmy Jack shit! The people gotta crown you. The people gotta say, that boy there is a bad mothafucka with that pen. It's not necessarily how many books you wrote, but how many books you wrote that the people were feeling. How many did you write that the people are saying are classic? Or are you a one-hit wonder? Only time can tell. And I, for one, believe you're only as good as your last book!

Now, I'm not saying I'm the best there ever was. I honestly don't think the best in this street lit/urban fiction genre even exists. There are entirely too many authors for there to be just one that's out here killing shit. I do believe there are but a handful of authors that's pimping the pen and giving you that work. There's not just one person that is the best, but there's a collective. An ensemble, if you will!

With that having been said, you pick any writer, from any generation, any subject, any plot, and pit them against your boy, Tha Ink Pen Pimp. I'm not saying I'ma fuck over them, but I'm telling you I'ma hold my own like a mothafucka! They may not be beat, but I guarantee they'll leave the fight licking their wounds.

-Peace, Tranay

The Last of the OGs 3

My Self-Published Works

The Devil Wears Timbs 1-7
Me and my Hittas 1-6
The Last Real Nigga Alive 1-3
A South Central Love Affair
A Hood Nigga's Blues

Tranay Adams

Chapter One

After putting Elgin's bitch ass to sleep, Hellraiser and the OGs went their separate ways with promises to link up later. Hellraiser returned to the hospital to spend the remainder of the night with his family. He came out of the elevator, made a left, and walked down the corridor. His aura screamed 'leave me the fuck alone, I'm going through some shit.' The hospital staff picked up on this. They whispered among each other as he walked past them. They wondered what was bothering him and thought of consoling him. But the spaced-out look in his eyes and the vibe was like repellant to them.

Hellraiser walked into KiMani's room and saw Lachaun sitting up in bed. She yawned and stretched her arms above her head. Her forehead creased when she saw him enter the room. She hopped off the bed and approached him.

"Baby, where you been?" Lachaun asked with concern.

Hellraiser didn't respond. He stood as still as a shit-stained statue in Central Park, with pigeons sitting on its head and shoulders.

"Treymaine, what's the matter?" Lachaun rephrased her question as she advanced toward him. The room was dark, so she could only make out his silhouette. It wasn't until she was two feet away that she could see his red-webbed eyes and the tears descending down his cheeks. She started to worry then.

Abruptly, Hellraiser hugged Lachaun and caught her off guard. He broke down sobbing as he held on to her. She didn't know what was going on with him, but she was sure she'd find out later. Right now, her husband wanted and needed to be comforted, so that's exactly what she was going to do to him.

"Shhhh. Shhhh," Lachaun shushed him as she hugged him. She kissed him on the cheek as she ran her hand up and down his back soothingly. "Everything is going to be okay, baby. I got chu. I got chu," she assured him, rocking him from side to side, continuously rubbing his back.

Hellraiser's tears were for the families of the men that had tried to kill KiMani. The thought of causing someone else's parents the same heartache as him and his wife brought him great sorrow. He was devastated and overwhelmed emotionally. Still, he wasn't going to let his sympathy for his opps' mother and father get in the way of him avenging his son. As far as he was concerned, the assassins that came after KiMani were dead men!

Hellraiser stared over Lachaun's shoulder as she held him in her arms. His forehead wrinkled when something caught his eye. He broke his wife's embrace and approached KiMani's bedside. Lachaun folded her arms across her chest and frowned, wondering what had her husband's attention.

"What's the matter, babe? What is it?" Lachaun asked him.

Hellraiser's forehead wrinkled further when he picked up the clear tube that supplied KiMani his oxygen. He examined it closely and saw a crease in it. Without taking his eyes off the tube, he motioned Lachaun over to him and showed it to her.

"What's up?" Lachaun asked, looking between him and the tube.

"Take a look at this," Hellraiser replied and pointed out the crease in it to her. "Was anyone in this room besides you and Billion?"

"Not that I know of. I mean, no one could have possibly come in here besides his nurse," Lachaun told him. She could see the worried look in his eyes, so she cupped his face and turned him to her. "Baby, what's the matter?"

The last thing I wanna do is have my baby stressing more than she already is. I'll just keep my thoughts to myself. Besides, I'm probably just thinking too far into things, Hellraiser thought with a slight smirk on his lips. "Nothing, baby, just tell the nurse to alert the staff to be a lil' more careful when they're working around the bed in here. One of them accidentally bent KiMani's tube. I don't know for sure, but he could have possibly have been without oxygen for a moment."

Lachaun looked at the crease in the tube and nodded under-standingly. "You're right, babe, I'm gonna go talk to them now." She kissed him and walked out of the room.

Hellraiser stood with his hands on his hips, looking at his son. Something told him the crease in the oxygen tube wasn't an accident. He had a hunch that an assassin had snuck into KiMani's room and deliberately tried to kill him.

**

When Niqua pulled back from kissing Assassin, she saw the gates of the mansion open and a white Chevrolet Tahoe heading their way. Assassin's brows crinkled, wondering what she was looking at, and he turned around. The Chevy truck parked on the white cobblestone driveway, and the driver killed its engine. The doors of the vehicle popped open and two men hopped out. Abrafo and Montez slammed the doors of the SUV and started over in Assassin and Niqua's direction. The king and queen of heroin lifted their protective eyewear to the top of their heads and waited for the killaz to approach.

"I take it y'all came bearing good news?" Assassin asked them and folded his arms across his chest.

"Yeah, both those lil' niggaz dead," Montez replied.

"Both of 'em? You sure about that?" Niqua inquired.

"Hell yeah," Montez said. "I was raised as a shooter, that shit is my m.o."

Assassin nodded understandingly. Montez did have a reputa-tion for busting his gun. His accuracy behind the trigger was second to none, which was why he'd recruited him. "You willing to bet your life on that, my nigga?"

Montez's brows wrinkled as he stared at Assassin. He glanced back at Abrafo to see what he had to say, but he didn't utter a word. So, he looked back at Assassin and nodded assuredly.

"Yeah, I'm willing to bet my life onnit. I stand behind my work," Montez replied confidently. "Look, I've been holding this piss since before we left to earth them lil' niggaz, I'm finna go use y'all bathroom." He patted Assassin on his shoulder and made his way toward the mansion, stepping over the debris of the statue.

Once Montez was out of sight, Assassin focused his attention on Abrafo. "Did Tez blow dem boyz down like he said he did?" Abrafo nodded. "You vouch for 'em being dead?" The silent hitta gave him a look that he read fluently. "Right. Well, if he didn't carry out my orders to the fullest, you know what to do with 'em, right?" Abrafo gave him another look that he read into. The African head hunter then stepped over the pieces of statue littering the lawn and headed toward the mansion.

"Alright, baby, let's get back to work," Assassin told Niqua as he took hold of his sledgehammer. The couple pulled their protective eyewear back down over their eyes, kissed, and went back to hammering away at what was left of Hitt-Man's statue.

Assassin knew all too well how easy it was to manipulate Niqua from watching his father's handling of her. She not only came from a broken home, but she suffered greatly from anxiety and depression. She desperately wanted to be loved and made to feel special by the opposite sex. Assassin took full advantage of this. He planned to use her just like his father had, and once he was done with her, he'd throw her away.

Assassin was going to play the role of the kind, caring, loving, and affectionate significant other to lower her guards. Then, once he knew without a doubt he was in her good graces, he was going to finesse the plug from her and take what his father built to another level.

Enjoy our time together while it lasts, sweetheart, 'cause it'll be coming to an end shortly, Assassin thought as he continued to destroy Hitt-Man's statue with his sledgehammer.

***

It was lights out in the men's correctional facility, so the convicts were either asleep, chopping it up with their celly, or wrapped up in their own thoughts. One particular hardened criminal occupied with mulling over his thoughts was Kyjuan. He was laid back on his bunk, picking the dirt out of his fingernails with a six-inch shank.

Ever since he'd taken the role of OG's top goon, he'd been eating like a fat rat in a cheese factory. He didn't want or need shit. The old head made sure his commissary stayed full, and he had a nice stash put away for a rainy day. Before he'd gotten locked up, he was putting in the same work out in the streets for a local drug baron that he was for OG. The only difference was, he was using a prison-made knife instead of his gun of choice, which was a .380 ACP. The crazy part about it was, he was making a more substantial amount of money inside than he was during his time on the streets. On top of that, he didn't really fuck with homie he was working for in the hood. It was all business for him. His relationship with OG was different. He really fucked with old dude. He'd shown him love since he'd touched the yard, making sure he had the necessities as well as the extras he wanted. And he didn't want a damn thing in return besides his loyalty.

Kyjuan and OG had grown significantly close since his incarceration. The old man treated him like he was his son and in turn, he respected him like he was his father. They were fucking with each other like they shared the same bloodline. In fact, they'd even gotten each other's name inked on them to solidify their family bond.

Feeling the vibration of his contraband cellphone in its hiding place, Kyjuan took the time to pull it out and hook up his earphones to it.

"Yo, hold on for a second," Kyjuan told the caller. He got off his bunk to see if OG was asleep. When he glanced at him, his eyes were closed and he was snoring softly. After he confirmed the old man was asleep, he settled back down on his bunk and started back picking his fingernails again. "What up? Nah, I hadda check to make sure my celly was asleep. I'm straight, loved one. I don't need shit. Like I told you before, the old man is keeping me well fed. Yes, sir." He nodded as he thought about the bankrolls of dirty money and commissary he was sitting on. "I'm right under 'em. A nigga done gained his trust, respect, and everything else. Believe me." He nodded and listened to what he was being told.

"I know you said that nigga Hellraiser is on the outside now. And when he finds out that we knocked off his son and his bitch-ass homeboy, he's gonna come seeking revenge," the caller assured him. "I don't give a fuck about that vow he made to God to live a non-violent life. He still has that gangsta shit in 'em, so he's gonna react. That old-ass nigga is gonna want blood. Best believe that."

"Facts."

"He and I are definitely gonna dance, and should I just so happen to be the one that loses, I want chu to take out the old man," the caller told him. "You think you can do that for me? Or should I get someone else to handle the job? I know you said you and that old nigga have grown close. I wouldn't want your feelings to get in the way of completing the task."

Kyjuan's heart started beating fast when the idea was brought up of him crushing OG. Though he fucked with the old man, he wasn't of his blood like the caller was.

"Yeah, I can do that," Kyjuan replied, still picking his finger-nails.

"Nigga, are you sure? If you can't, I gotta couple of animals on the inside that don't mind getting bloody."

"I'ma handle it. Don't even worry about it."

"Thata boy," the caller said jovially. "Look here, I'ma make it worth yo' while. How does twenty gees sound? I can have that dropped off to yo' BM with no problem. Shit, as a matter of fact, you good for it, bro. I can hit her with that purse tonight."

"Nah, don't sweat it. You took care of me since I touched down in here," Kyjuan reminded the caller. "If I'ma do this, then I'ma do it on the love."

"My nigga, love," the caller said happily.

"Love. Peace." Kyjuan disconnected the call, powered off his jack, and stashed it back in its hiding place. He then held up the shank before his eyes and imagined himself putting it through OG's chest. His mind was bombarded with images of the old man

14

wincing and hollering in pain. The thought of inflicting so much pain on a nigga brought him great joy. He was a killa at heart. So, the anticipation of putting in work excited him like new pussy.

***

Zekey pulled up in the driveway of his house and killed the engine of his truck. He, Quan, and Ali hopped out, making their way across the front lawn. He hung his arms around their necks as they proceeded to the front door of their home. They were ignorant to the presence of the van parked directly across the street from them. It had been outside their crib for hours, waiting for someone to come home. Its occupants were five masked gunmen dressed in all black, with night-vision goggles sitting at the top of their heads. They were busy loading their machine guns, when Zekey and his family had arrived. Each man present and accounted for was more dangerous than the next. They were all coldblooded killaz and pledged their loyalty to one man—Changa—Travieso's uncle.

"Okay, they're inside. Let's go," the driver said to the killaz in Spanish. He had just seen Zekey and his family go in the house and shut the door.

All the masked gunmen hopped out the van and crouched down. Together, they hurriedly made their way across the street, looking in both directions.

The Grim Reaper had arrived to claim the lives of Zekey and his family. And the sad part about it was, they didn't even know he was coming.

The masked hittaz invaded Zekey's front yard with the driver, Francisco, leading their pack. He signaled to the others to take their position while he and two of them made their way on the side of the house. The hittaz played the role of lookout while Francisco drew his hunting knife. Using the blade, he popped open the fuse box and then severed the wires that provided electricity to the entire house. As soon as he was done, he sheathed the hunting knife and motioned for his comrades to follow him. They ran to the backdoor of the house while hearing the rest of their team kicking in the front door. Thirty seconds later, they were kicking open the backdoor and flooding the house.

Francisco and his hittaz made their way inside the kitchen, looking through their night-vision goggles and swaying their machine guns around. The atmosphere of the entire house was creepy and deathly quiet, besides the ticking of the grandfather clock inside the living room. Unbeknownst to the three men, there was a shadowy figure moving in the background of them. Quietly, he pulled a butcher's knife out of the knife block and bit down on it. He removed a meat cleaver and a big fork. He tucked the fork inside of his belt, hunched down, and crept up behind the last masked hitta, with the meat cleaver at the ready.

The shadowy figure was actually Zekey. He came behind the last masked hitta, yanking his head back by his chin and slicing his throat with the meat cleaver. Instantly, blood poured out of the slit in his neck, and his eyes rolled to the back of his head. Zekey quickly pulled him back into the darkness and slumped him against the wall, out of sight. With his sights set on the masked hittaz behind Francisco, Zekey crept up behind him as fast as he could, but the squeaking of the kitchen floor alerted him to Zekey's presence. The masked hitta whipped around to open fire, but by then, he was too late. Zekey pounced on him with the vigor and grace of a lioness, snatching his big fork from out of his belt. Grunting, he slammed the fork into his left eye socket with all his might.

"Aaaaaah!" the masked hitta hollered out at the top of his lungs and discharged his machine gun at the floor. Zekey charged him into the wall, with the big fork still in his eye socket. Upon impact, the fork went through the back of his skull, knocking a portrait down, and nailed his head against the wall. The masked hitta went limp and hung from the wall like a shirt would from a hanger in the closet. At this time, the rest of the masked hittaz inside of the living room were running toward the kitchen and shouting shit in Spanish Zekey couldn't quite understand. Zekey took the butcher's knife from between his teeth as Francisco was attempting to lift his machine gun. Before he could pull its trigger, the butcher's knife was spinning at him so fast it was a blur.

"Gaaaahhh!" Francisco screamed in great pain as blood spurted out of his chest. He dropped his machine gun and grabbed the butcher's knife by its handle. He attempted to pull it out, but Zekey kicked the knife's hilt hard and fast. The impact from the blow buried the knife into Francisco's chest down to its handle, killing him instantly. Swiftly, Zekey scooped up two of his victims' machine guns and pulled Francisco's cadaver into him. He whipped around with both the automatic weapons up, spitting flames at the opposition while their bullets pelted Francisco's dead body.

Buratatatatatatatat!

The first masked hitta running up on Zekey busting caught a chest full of some hot shit and fell to his bloody death. The last two masked hittaz were coming at Zekey fast, sending heat in his direction. Zekey tossed the empty automatic weapons aside, pushed Francisco's lifeless form off him, and dove to the floor. He narrowly missed the automatic gunfire that was meant to take his life. Zekey kicked the kitchen table over onto its side and revealed two semi-automatic handguns duct taped underneath it. He snatched them off and got back up to his feet. He could hear the booted steps of the other masked hittaz getting closer and closer to the kitchen. The masked hittaz were so focused on the ex-dopefiend that they neglected their surroundings, which would prove to be fatal. Hidden in the dark corner of the living room was Ali. He was down on his knees with a fishing line wrapped around both of his gloved hands. He waited until the masked hittaz were about to cross the threshold into the kitchen, and then he pulled the line hard.

Boiiing!

The line straightened, and the masked hittaz tripped over it clumsily. They fell to the floor, and their machine guns went up in the air. Zekey came charging out of the kitchen, and Quan, gripping an AR-15, came from out of the living room closet. They met each other in the kitchen doorway and pointed their weapons at the masked hittaz. The men's eyes lit up, and they went to scream. Before the sound could escape their mouths, the married couple unloaded on that ass mercilessly.

Buratatatatatatat!

Poc, poc, poc, poc, poc!

Zekey and Quan pumped bullets upon bullets into the masked hittaz, which made them do a funny dance on the floor. Ali remained on his knees where he was with a scrunched up face and his hands covering his ears. The sound of the reoccurring machine gun fire was awfully loud and made his eardrums feel like they were going to burst.

Zekey tucked his warm, smoking guns on his waistline and pulled Quan into him. Holding her by her waist, he kissed her loud and passionately.

"Good job, mamas," Zekey told her, with sweat peppering his forehead. He was breathing hard and his adrenaline was starting to wear off. He motioned for Ali, and he came right over. "You did good, son, real good. I'm proud of you." He dapped him up and he cracked a grin. Quan smiled at him and ruffled his head. She hated the fact that he had to get involved in something so bloody, but understood that his hand was needed in protecting their family. "As a matter of fact, I'm proud of both of y'all. Y'all did the damn thang tonight."

"Thanks goes to baby boy," Quan said with a grin and hung her arm around Ali's shoulders. "If it wasn't for 'em spotting that van when we drove up, these fools"—she took the time to kick one of the dead hittaz in the head—"may have gotten the drop on us." She kissed her son on the side of his head and hugged him into her.

"Alright, y'all, no time to waste," Zekey said as he smacked and rubbed his hands together. "Let's move these bad boys to the bathroom so we can drain 'em and chop they asses up," he told them, looking around at all the dead bodies. "Oh, yeah, it's gonna be a looooong night."

Right then, a cellphone rang. The Whitmores exchanged glances and shrugged. They didn't know whose cellular was ringing, but it wasn't either of theirs. Listening closely, Zekey followed the ringing device. It stopped ringing and then it started up again.

"I think—" Ali started, but was quickly cut short by Zekey holding up his hand.

Ali and Quan watched as Zekey made his way over to the masked hitta whose head he'd nailed to the wall with the big fork. He patted down his body until he felt something shaped like a rectangle. He pulled out what was a cellphone and looked at the screen. There was a telephone number on its display, but it wasn't programmed under a name. Someone was trying to Facetime the dead man. Zekey wasn't for sure who was calling, but he had a clue.

Zekey accepted the video call and smiled wickedly at the caller, who looked shocked to see him. The caller was Travieso's sixty-seven-year-old uncle Changa. He was one of the bosses of a very feared and prominent cartel in Mexico, and his reach didn't have any limitations. He had a nest of graying hair and a receding hairline that made his forehead look bigger in appearance. A black leather eye-patch was secured over his left eye, and its strap was snug around his head. He had a bushy mustache that curled over his top lip and a five o'clock shadow. He was dressed in a long-sleeve, silk shirt, and it was opened to his fluffy gray chest hair. At first glance, one would assume he was your everyday elderly Mexican man, but looks were deceiving. The gentleman staring back at Zekey was ruthless, conniving, and as dangerous as they come.

"What up, Changa? Yo' old ass look like you've seen a ghost," Zekey said. "I know you're probably wondering where's that hit squad you sent for me, so lemme show 'em to you." He walked around the house, showing him the dead bodies of every one of his hittaz. Then he looked back at the display so the cartel boss could see his face. "You missed, homes, and I'ma make you pay for that." Zekey scowled and pointed his finger at Changa.

Changa was seething mad. His face turned red and veins bulged on his forehead. "Fucking, mayate, I'll chop off your head and use it as a salsa bowl!"

"Suck my dick, old man!" Zekey said furiously and spat a loogey on the cellphone's screen. He held up the middle finger at Changa, dropped the cellular at his foot, and stomped and ground it into the floor. The pressure underneath his sneaker cracked the device's display into a cobweb and distorted its picture. "Alright, son, you go downstairs in the basement and get the hatchet and saw for me," he told Ali. "Me and ya momma will start carrying these dead spics upstairs to the bathroom. Now, go, go, go, go! We don't have time to waste." He clapped his hands, hurrying Ali along. The boy ran to the basement door, snatched it open, and hurried down the staircase. By the time he was halfway down the steps, his mother and stepfather were carrying Francisco's body up the stairs.

Chapter Two

Once the Whitmores had gotten rid of the dead bodies, they cleaned up the house and packed their bags. They knew they couldn't stay at their home anymore since Changa had found out where they lived. So, they checked into the Ritz-Carlton hotel in downtown Los Angeles. Zekey got a two-bedroom suite so Ali would have his own bedroom and space to lounge. They sat at the kitchen table like a family and ate the fast food from Wendy's they bought on their way over. After they'd finished eating, Ali hugged and kissed his mother goodnight and dapped up Zekey before retiring to his bedroom for a good night's sleep.

Zekey and Quan showered together and took care of their hygiene. They dried off with their towels and hung them up on the back of the bathroom door. They then walked into their bedroom as naked as Adam and Eve were in the Garden of Eden. Zekey picked up the remote control, turned on the flat-screen television, and turned the volume up. He tossed the remote control upon the dresser and pulled Quan into him. She wrapped her arms around his neck while he held her waist. They made out with their eyes closed while the light from the TV shone on their nude bodies.

The couple's kissing turned them both on and had them exceptionally aroused. Zekey's dick was as hard as an Olympic runner's baton, while Quan's pussy was wet and sticky. Zekey rubbed up and down her great big ass. He pulled her huge butt cheeks apart, groped them, and then smacked each one of them. He then kissed Quan down her body, got down on her knees, and kept kissing her till he reached her stomach. There were black stretch marks on either side of her belly from when she was pregnant with Ali, but he didn't give a fuck. He loved anything and everything about her, even her flaws. This was because they were all a part of her. So, how could he not love everything that made up the woman he loved most in the whole wide world?

Zekey tenderly kissed each of Quan's stretch marks. Smiling, she stared down at him while rubbing his bald head. A tingly sensation stirred in her southern region as he gently bit on her fupa and rubbed her chubby thighs. Her twat leaked like the roof of an old house on a rainy day. He tapped the inside of her left thigh, and she placed her bare left foot on the bed. Cupping her buttocks, he nestled his nose into her coochie while keeping his eyes closed. He inhaled her natural scent as if it was a lily he'd plucked from a beautiful garden on a 75-degree summer day. He loved the smell of her pussy. It was something about its usual smell that really got him going. His dick had gotten even harder then in that moment, and he couldn't wait to taste her jewel.

Zekey licked Quan from her crinkle between her pussy lips and sucked on her clitoris like it was a piece of butterscotch candy. She threw her head up, her eyes narrowed, and her mouth hung open. She passionately clawed at Zekey's bald head and sucked her left tittie. As Zekey sucked on the small flap of meat between her lower lips, he stuck two fingers inside of her and moved his hand faster and faster into her.

"Uh, uh, uh, uh, oh, oh, oh, shiiii—shiiit, baby!" Frowning, Quan looked down at Zekey while constantly rubbing his bald head. She could feel herself nearing a sexual explosion as her husband manipulated her sex. "Oh, oh, oh, oh, my *God*—oh, my *God*—right there! Don't stop, baby, please don't stop! I swear to God, if you stop, I'ma fucking kill you!" she cried literally. Tears flowed freely down her chubby face, and she began to tremble. Suddenly, Zekey shoved his thumb into her butthole, and she jumped with a startle. It was unexpected, but it intensified the orgasm she felt coming on. "Ooooou! Here I come, baby! Here I— here I—here I fucking cummmmmm!" She threw her head back and screamed louder than that fat white lady at the opera. Her engorged pussy lips erupted and drenched Zekey, but his old freaky ass kept on going. He kept sucking on her jewel, finger fucking her, and thumbing her anus. She stumbled backwards trying to maintain her balance while pushing him off her. Finally, he released her and she dropped to the floor. She hugged her knees to her breasts and bowed her head. She moaned as she shivered like she was naked outside in the middle of a Chicago winter.

Zekey stood over her, stroking his piece up and down while staring down at her. His shit was incredibly hard and ready for action.

"Hold on, baby, I know you ain't done yet. We're just getting started," Zekey said with a one-sided, devilish smirk. Quan looked back up at him, smiling devilishly as well. She stuck her wet tongue at him and coiled it back and forth. It was like she was telling him to come here with it. She got down on her knees before him, holding her mouth open. She groped her breasts and tweaked her thick nipples. Although her twat was contracting and oozing from her orgasm, she required more of her husband. Her body was fiending for him in every way imaginable. All the violence earlier that night didn't even damper her sex drive. It did the exact opposite. Seeing her man handle Changa's hittaz back at their house proved he was a provider and a protector. His display of masculinity naturally made her submissive to him, and she eagerly wanted to be dominated by him. She desperately wanted him in her pussy, her ass, and in her mouth—every hole in her body.

Zekey grabbed Quan by her head and shoved himself between her lips. He gently thrust her mouth, making her gag and choke on him. Looking up at him, she flicked her clitoris rapidly and massaged her man's dangling nutsack. He groaned and basked in the sensational feeling of her delicate touch. It started feeling so euphoric to him that he placed his right foot on top of the dresser and planted his left foot firmly on the floor for leverage. He then started fucking her mouth, going as deep and as hard as he could and making her ass gag. Tears ran out of Quan's eyes and bubbly saliva poured out of her mouth. The slimy saliva hung from her chin like gold rope chains, and some of it broke apart and splattered on the floor.

"Awww, fuck, baby—umm—shit! Yo' mouth feels so good!" Zekey said with his eyes closed, clenching and unclenching his jaws. He could feel the engorged head of his dick grazing the back of her throat and causing friction. The shit was driving him crazy and egging him to bust.

"Gag, ack, ack, gag, ack, ack!" Quan made explicit noises as her mouth was being fucked. Her eyes were bucked and tears streamed down her cheeks. More of the bubbly saliva built up inside her mouth, spilled out, and hung like ropes from her chin.

"Uh, uh, uh, uh!" Zekey said aloud with his head tilted back. He was gripping Quan's head like it was a basketball while he fucked her mouth recklessly. His muscular buttocks were moving back and forth super-fast while his nutsack smacked against her chin. He knew he was about to cum, but he wasn't ready to yet. He wanted some pussy before he got off.

Zekey pulled out of Quan's mouth with slimy globs of her saliva hanging from his dick. Quan spat on the carpeted floor and wiped her wet mouth with her hand. Without saying a word, Zekey instructed her to get on the bed and spread her legs open. She climbed up on the bed like he'd instructed, but she interlocked her ankles behind her head. Zekey, while stroking his piece, smiled when she did this, and she smiled back. She teased him with her long tongue and licked her lips. Her pussy was wide enough for him to see its pink walls, and her asshole was the size of a quarter. He loved how they both looked sitting out there in front of him.

"Damn, that shit looks good as fuck, mamas. I've gotta taste alla that before I bust you down," Zekey told her as he stood there stroking himself up and down. The skin on his dick wrinkled and straightened with each stroke, and a clear fluid seeped out of his peehole.

Zekey dropped to his knees, licking and sucking on Quan's butthole while stimulating her clitoris. Her eyes crossed and her mouth flung open. She whimpered and moaned, hearing him devour her anus and toy with her clit. Her twat contracted like she was trying to exert a baby, and her essence flowed freely from it.

"Mmmmmmummmmm," Zekey murmured while feasted on her asshole sloppily. Her butt had been lubricated from his excessive spit and contracting as well. Using his tongue as a spear, he jabbed it in and out of her gaping hole. His playing with her brown eye and stimulating her treasure had her hollering and gripping the covers. Before she knew it, she was screaming to the heavens in bliss and transforming into a human water fountain. Her fluid shot into the air and rained down on her husband.

Zekey wiped his dripping chin and climbed into the bed. He squatted over Quan, and she watched him push his swollen dick head inside of her. She gasped, feeling him fill her up inch by inch. He closed his eyes and licked his lips as he leaned forward, placing his fists on either side of his wife. His ass was tooted up in the air with his butthole on display. The muscles in his arms, back, and buttocks flexed as he thrust downward. He dropped dick deep down inside of her. His nutsack smacked down against her crinkle with each of his thrusts. Her twat spilled her essence and ran down onto the sheet below.

"Yeah, yeah, yeah," Zekey said under his breath while slamming down into Quan. The force he was dropping upon her shook the bed and made its springs cry. Quan's sensual whining mixed with the high volume of the television set. Her eyes were closed, her head was bouncing up and down and so were her enormous breasts. She held her man's waist with one hand and used the other to massage her clit. Her face balled up, and she flicked his left nipple with her tongue. She then started sucking on it like a thirsty baby. Little mama was multitasking, sucking his nipple while stimulating her clitoris.

"Oh, oh, oh, I'm finna—I'm finna have an—an orgasm, baaaaeeeeee!" Quan's eyes exploded open and she screamed to the top of her lungs.

"I'm 'bouta cum in this pussy too," Zekey said, placing his mouth over Quan's and kissing her deeply. He then threw his head back up, slammed deep down into her three more times, and ground hard into her. His warm semen splashed against her internal walls, and she orgasmed right after. Her pussy overflowed and flooded the sheets. She shook uncontrollably and bit down on her bottom lip. She took her ankles from behind her head, and he lay on top of her. They kissed sensually and romantically.

Zekey rolled off of Quan and laid flat on his back with his arms and legs spread. Quan snuggled up to him and threw her leg over his waist. She nibbled on his earlobe while rubbing his left pectoral muscle, which had *Rest in Peace, Dorothea* inked on it. Dorothea was his mother who'd died from natural causes during his last stint in prison.

Zekey smiled with his eyes closed, feeling his wife nibbling on his ear and then gradually moving to kissing on his slightly hairy chest. He could feel himself getting hard again, so he turned her over on her back and they went at it once more. Afterwards, they showered again and got dressed for bed. Zekey left their bedroom door open and tucked a gun underneath his and Quan's pillows. Though the Whitmores were way in downtown L.A. with security on deck at a luxurious hotel, he still made sure to be strapped. For all he knew, Changa's hittaz could find some way to sneak their asses up there to assassinate him and his family.

"So, what's the agenda tomorrow, hubby?" Quan asked, lying on her side with Zekey holding her. His eyes were closed and his forehead was pressed against the back of her head. She enjoyed the feeling of his hot breath tickling the back of her neck hairs. She loved being in his arms. It was the most comfortable and safe place there was on Earth to her.

"We drop off a bag for Arnez's funeral arrangements," Zekey told her. "Then we see about hollering at that nigga, Hell. We have a common enemy, so I figure we should join forces and squash 'em."

"I agree, but aren't chu worried how he's gonna take you? I mean, he doesn't know you like that, and should he find out about you setting up his son and then trying to off him back at the hospital—baby, I really think you should refrain from coming into contact with 'em at all," Quan told him with her head turned to her side.

"Baby, you're worrying too much. I got this," Zekey assured her and kissed the back of her neck affectionately.

"Okay, baby. I trust you." Quan took a breath. She used the remote to turn off the television and then sat it aside. She snuggled up against Zekey and held his arm. "I love you."

"Not nearly as much as I love you," Zekey replied and tightened his hold on her.

***

The Next Day

Big Craig, a big, fat, black, baldhead dude who walked with a limp, made his way down the hallway mopping the floor. Occasionally, he'd check his surroundings as he performed the task. Ever since he'd ass betted OG, he'd been making excuses about why he couldn't pay him and avoiding anyone associated with him. He knew that being in prison, he couldn't avoid the throwback gangsta and his top goon, Kyjuan, for long. He'd have to grow eyes at the back of his head, but that was impossible. So, he knew his fate would come down to him being on the bad end of a shank. Mindful of this, he was sure to keep a banga on him at all times so he'd be prepared whenever drama rose.

Big Craig busied himself with thoughts of a story he could sell to his mother so she would send him some money to pay OG off. He'd become so consumed with his thoughts he neglected his surroundings and was oblivious to the presence of death lurking nearby. His eyes widened with fear and his mouth flung open. Through the reflection of the wet floor, he'd seen someone creeping up on him with something shiny and deadly in their hand.

"Oh, shit!" Big Craig said aloud. He dropped the handle of the mop, and it deflected off the floor. He whipped around to his would-be attacker and reached for the piece of sharp steel in his waistline. He'd cleared it halfway from where he'd hid it when Kyjuan kicked it out of his hand. Kyjuan pulled him close, like he was a broad and he wanted to kiss him. Holding eye contact with him, he snarled like the beast he was and brought his ice pick-like shank into play.

"OG wanted you to have this, fat boy!" Kyjuan said with hostility dripping from his every word. Holding Big Craig tight, he jabbed him with his pick so fast, his hand was a blur. The big man howled in pain, and he reached for Kyjuan's face. Kyjuan turned his head and continued to poke his ass up! The hateful look on his face made him look like he'd been possessed by a demon.

Kyjuan could see himself in Big Craig's pupils as he repeatedly assaulted him. The big man gasped for breaths loudly and his mouth quivered, blood spilling down his chin. Kyjuan poked him thirty more times, twisted his pick inside of him, and then pushed him down to the floor. He looked up and down the hallway for any witnesses as he cleaned his fingerprints from his weapon on Big Craig's shirt. Kyjuan tossed the bloody knife to the floor and walked away whistling, like he hadn't done shit.

Big Craig lay where he was on the floor, wide eyed and coughing up blood. He clutched at the bloody wounds in his chest and wheezed. The more blood that filled his punctured lungs, the more of it he coughed up. He turned on his side and extended his bloody finger to the wall. Using his very own blood as ink, he began to write the name of his killa. He managed to write K, Y, and J before his spirit left his body and he took his last breath. Fortunately for Kyjuan, the clue he left as to who his murderer was wouldn't be enough to connect him to the slaying.

***

Next Day/Evening

Hellraiser and Lachaun walked out of the funeral home, scratching their heads. They'd gone to pay for the services for Arnez's funeral, but to their surprise, the bill had already been paid. For the life of them, they couldn't figure out who could have dropped the bread for the expenses. And trying to figure it out was driving them crazy.

"Soooo, what do you say we do with this fat check, handsome?" Lachaun asked as she walked beside Hellraiser, her arm interlocked with his. Her eyes were focused on the check pinched between her fingers. It was the first half of the payment they'd made to the home for Arnez's arrangements. It had been reimbursed since the anonymous payee settled their tab in full.

"Uhh, shit, I don't know, babe. What do you suggest?" Hellraiser replied, looking over at her as he pulled out his car keys.

"Well, I had my eye on this property over in Ladera Heights," Lachaun told him. "I think this will make a good down payment on—"

"Mr. and Mrs. James, though it is a pleasure to meet chu, I wish it was under better circumstances," a deep, masculine voice said, garnering their attention. They looked up and saw the likes of Zekey. They couldn't quite see his face thanks to it being minutes before sunset. However, they could make out his bald head and custom attire. He was sporting an overcoat over a fitted, tailor-made suit and skinny tie. His hands were tucked in the pockets of his slacks. A gust of wind made the end of his overcoat flap in mid-air and caused debris to encircle him.

Hellraiser and Lachaun exchanged glances like, *who the fuck is this*? They then looked back at Zekey. Hellraiser, feeling the man before them posed a threat, stepped in front of Lachaun to shield her from any harm.

"I'm sorry, but do we know you, homie?" Hellraiser asked, with a creased forehead.

"I'm Ezekiel, but you can call me Zekey or Zeek," Zekey replied. He was standing unbelievably still while the end of his overcoat continued to flap in mid-air. "You've gotta few years on me, but we know some of the same people. Hell, we're from the same hood. I'm surprised you haven't heard of me."

"Zekey, Zekey, Zekey," Lachaun repeated to herself over and over again. She was holding her big hat on her head so the wind wouldn't blow it off and holding her coat closed. While she was trying to recall where she'd heard the name 'Zekey' before, Hellraiser was listening closely. Still, he kept his unwavering eye on the man standing in front of him.

It clicked in Lachaun's head where she'd heard Zekey's name before. Her eyes bulged and her mouth flung open. "I remember him, babe. KiMani told me about a beef he'd had with 'em back in the day. They were all gung-ho trying to kill each other."

Upon hearing Zekey had been trying to kill his son, Hellraiser mad dogged him and upped his gun. He pointed it right between his eyes. Lachaun was right behind him, pulling her gun from her purse and pointing it at Zekey. Zekey didn't seem moved by the guns being pointed at him. He remained calm and cool.

"Is this true? You tried to take out my boy?" Hellraiser asked him, with murder twinkling in his eyes.

"I was told you only lie to someone you're afraid of," Zekey told him. "So, yeah, I tried to take his lil' ass out."

"Wrong answer, homeboy," Hellraiser replied, cocking the hammer of his blower with his thumb.

"I tried to murder yo' boy when he was just twelve years old," Zekey went on to tell him. "Then, again, a couple of nights ago while he was lying inna coma at the hospital."

Hellraiser's mind flashed back to the night he'd found the crease mark in KiMani's breathing tube. He thought it was strange, and now he knew who'd made the move against him.

"When I entered the room, he wasn't the only one there," Zekey said. "Your wife and who I gather was yo' youngest son were lying asleep in the bed on the other side of the room."

Hellraiser and Lachaun narrowed their eyes, wondering why he was telling them what he was, and why hadn't he killed KiMani while he had the chance.

"Why didn't you finish the job?" Hellraiser asked curiously.

"Arnez. I loved that boy like he was my flesh and blood," Zekey replied. "And I knew that by turning yo' boy's lights out would be like killing him all over again."

"He coulda killed me and Billion," Lachaun said in a hushed tone to Hellraiser. He nodded understandingly but kept his eyes and gun on Zekey.

"I coulda taken your entire family along for the ride, but I let that beef I had witcho son die," Zekey informed him. "I let it die right along with Arnez."

"What chu got up yo' sleeve, my nigga?" Hellraiser asked. "You tryna set a trap for me or something?"

"Homie, if I wanted you dead I could make that happen right now," Zekey told him in a playful voice. It sounded like he wanted to laugh to Hellraiser and Lachaun. "What, y'all don't believe me?

I got six snipers planted all around this bitch." He looked around as he motioned with his finger.

"Bullshit, I say you're bluffing," Hellraiser said.

"I'm with my man, prove it," Lachaun chimed in.

"Alright," Zekey replied.

Hellraiser and Lachaun saw him place a finger inside his ear and whisper to something they couldn't see. Their heads were on a swivel, expecting someone or something to come, but nothing came. The next thing Lachaun knew, her big hat was snatched off her head. Her eyes widened with surprise and she looked behind herself. Her hat was being carried away by the wind. It tumbled on the ground and landed against the back tire of a nearby parked car. A bullet hole was visible in it.

Lachaun turned back around to Hellraiser. "Baby, he's not bullshitting. There's really a sniper out there somewhere.

"Still think I'm pulling yo' chain, my nigga? Hol' up," Zekey said something else in a whisper. Shortly, Lachaun's gold loop earring exploded from her earlobe, and the strap of her purse came apart. Her purse dropped to the ground and spilled its contents. She knew from the whizzing near her ear and purse there were bullets being fired at her.

"Alright. Let's say I believe you," Hellraiser told him. "What's next?"

"You accept my invitation to Arnez's funeral," Zekey told him and pulled out a card with the information on it. "I know he would have wanted you and your family there." Hellraiser stared at the card for a moment before plucking it from Zekey's fingers and lowering his gun. He studied the card before sliding it into his pocket. "Oh, yeah, I almost forgot." He pulled a folded up newspaper from out of his overcoat and passed it to Hellraiser.

"What's this?" Hellraiser frowned as he took the newspaper. When he opened it up, Hitt-Man's face was on the front page, with a headline: KINGPIN MURDERED IN A GANGLAND-STYLE HIT. Hellraiser couldn't believe his eyes. Someone had smoked Hitt-Man before he had the chance to do it himself. "You know whose work this is?"

"Notta clue," Zekey told him. "But now that he's outta the way, I'm sure his son is gonna fill his shoes."

"Who is the nigga's son?" Hellraiser asked, passing the newspaper to Lachaun for her to look at it.

"Assassin," Zekey reported. "He sent his flunkies at me with ten stacks for the whereabouts of KiMani. I dropped them the line, and our boys got hit."

"Wait a minute, you mean it's your fault Arnez is dead and KiMani's laid up in the hospital?" Lachaun said heatedly as she walked ahead of Hellraiser, smacking his hand down when he tried to grab her arm.

"Like I told you before, you only lie to those you're afraid of," Zekey said. "And I'm not afraid of anyone."

"Well, is that a yes or a no?" Lachaun asked as she gripped her gun tighter.

Zekey was quiet for a minute before he answered her question. "Yes."

Whack!

Lachaun struck him across the side of his head with her piece. He stumbled to the side, holding the side of his bleeding head.

"Hold your fire! Hold your fire!" Zekey shouted to one of the snipers through his ear bud, dripping blood on the collar of his shirt. He looked back up at Lachaun, wincing and understanding her pain. "I'ma hold that one, lil' mama, 'cause I deserve it. I can't front. If it hadn't been for me, then Arnez would still be alive," he said with teary eyes that made Lachaun feel sorry for him. She came to the conclusion that he didn't need her beating on him since he already felt bad enough. With that in mind, she stashed her gun inside of her purse and walked back over to Hellraiser. "Look, Hell, if you plan on bringing it to these fools responsible for the shooting, then I want in on it. Them boys didn't just take my nephew, they took my best fucking friend."

"I'll keep you in mind," Hellraiser assured him. Zekey extended his hand to him. Hell looked at it like he'd just scratched his ass with it, and then he hesitantly shook it. "Come on, baby." He interlocked his fingers with Lachaun's, and they walked over to their whip. Zekey stood with his hands in his pockets and his coat still flapping in mid-air. He watched as the couple pulled out of their parking space and then drove off.

A minute later, a big ass SUV drove with its headlights illuminating Zekey. He walked over to the front passenger door and hopped inside, slamming the door behind him. Ali was behind the wheel. He wasn't old enough to drive yet, but he knew how from his biological father showing him. He was wearing an ear bud in his ear and had a gun with a silencer on his lap. Although his mother didn't approve of him being in the middle of his stepfather's dealings, Zekey worked his magic on her and convinced her to go against her better judgment. Besides, the boy was nearly an adult, and he had a hand in murking one of the niggaz while defending their home.

"Really, Pop? Six shooters?" Ali said with a smile, as he made a left and went in the opposite direction. "You know damn well there isn't anyone out there besides Moms."

"Aye, sometimes you gotta overexaggerate in case niggaz wanna try you," Zekey told him, taking the time to fire up a cigarette. It was a nasty habit he'd picked up in prison since he'd given up snorting dope.

"I feel you." Ali nodded as he drove up on his mother. She stashed her sniper rifle inside a secret compartment inside the hatch of the truck, along with a pistol. Next, she slammed the hatch shut and hopped into the backseat of the SUV. As soon as she was safely inside, Ali drove away.

Unbeknownst to everyone that had left the grounds of the cemetery, parked three rows back in a limousine-tinted vehicle was Abrafo watching the entire exchange. An hour prior, he had a meeting with the funeral director and a couple of his workers. A few palms were greased and an agreement was made.

"Yeah, they just pulled out of here—" Abrafo said to the cellphone mounted on the dashboard.

"Yo, boss dog, we can slide up on 'em right quick and lay 'em all down. You just give the word," Vato interjected from the front passenger seat with a carbine lying across his lap. His box braids spilled from underneath a black baseball cap. Black sunglasses concealed his eyes, a black bandana was around his neck cowboy style, and black gloves covered his hands. Vato was a seventeen-year-old, half-Belizean, half-Mexican kid, fresh out of youth authority, and eager to prove himself within the organization. Although he was a low-level foot soldier, Assassin saw great potential within him. This was why he'd picked him to pair with Abrafo, out of a handful of savage animals dying to bust their guns for him.

Abrafo looked at Vato with annoyance for yelling so closely to his ear. If looks could kill, the junior head buster would have dropped dead on the spot.

"My fault, big homie," Vato told him, seeing he'd frustrated him. "What do you say, jefe? Let us know before these fools getta way."

There was a moment of silence before Assassin spoke again.

"Y'all niggaz fall back, Blood, the sun still out," Assassin reminded them. "Catching them bodies isn't worth that much to me if it's gonna cost me two of my best hittaz. Know what I mean?"

Vato looked disappointed that Assassin didn't want them to splash Hellraiser and them. He was addicted to the drama and craved to lie something down.

"Yeah, I got it," Vato replied with disappointment dripping from his vocal cords. He lowered his carbine to the floor at his booted feet and slumped down in his seat. He then plucked what was left of a blunt out of the ashtray, sparked that bitch up, and blew out a smoke cloud.

"Stop being so eager, my young nigga, you'll getta chance to make your bones," Assassin assured him. "I promise you that. As a matter of fact, I gotta nigga I want chu to holla at real soon."

A smile stretched across Vato's blackish lips, which he'd acquired from smoking so much weed over the years. He sat up in his seat and tried to pass the bleezy to Abrafo, but he waved him off. The foreign killa didn't get high nor did he drink. He believed in one treating their body as if it were a temple.

"Oh, yeah? Who are we talking about, boss dog?" Vato asked excitedly as he snuffed out his blunt inside the ashtray.

"You'll see, lil' homie, you just gotta be patient," Assassin told him.

"Alright. Bet." Vato grinned and rubbed his hands together in anticipation.

"Smooth," Assassin replied and disconnected the call.

Abrafo cranked up the whip and backed out of the parking space. He then looked both ways before driving out into Los Angeles traffic.

Tranay Adams

Chapter Three
Night

Abrafo, shirtless and holding a gun in his hand, stood before his dresser mirror, looking himself over. He had light-brown eyes, hair in short twists, and a goatee with a few graying hairs. Though his dark-chocolate body was covered in muscles, it bore many scars from his dangerous profession. He admired every keloid scar and old stab wound. They collectively reminded him of how much of a warrior he was. He wore them proudly like a marine wore the medals he'd earned during his service to his country.

Abrafo's hand traveled over the hideous scars on his body, and his mind was hit with back-to-back visuals of how he'd gotten each one. He shut his eyes for a moment and allowed himself to be transported back to those times. He had resorted to a level of savagery he didn't know he had in him, to save his life. During his climb up the ladder in the murder game, he had been both predator and prey. Needless to say, he favored being in the position of the predator over all else.

Feeling someone walking up behind him, Abrafo's eyes popped open and he saw his wife, Tulip, slipping a beige Kevlar bulletproof vest over his head. As he began strapping the body armor on, she slipped a gris-gris Voodoo amulet necklace around his neck and fastened it. The gris-gris was believed to bring its wearer luck and protection from evil. Once Tulip fastened the necklace around Abrafo's neck, she went on to help him get dressed for the night's mission. He slipped on his black T-shirt, hooded duster, gloves, and pocketed his ski mask. Afterwards, he tucked the guns Tulip brought him in his shoulder holsters and placed a few automatic weapons inside of a long black duffle bag. Abrafo snatched up the duffle bag, tucked his car keys, and pulled Tulip into him. He kissed her forehead and her lips.

Abrafo looked Tulip in the eyes as she wrapped her arms around his neck. She was a shade lighter than him and she rocked a reddish-brown fade. Her eyes were slanted like she was Korean. She had a large, flat nose and fat, succulent lips. Her facial features made her look extremely exotic and alluring. Her beauty, her curves, enormous boobs, and big ass made her a sight to see. Like Abrafo, she had tribal scars on her forehead, cheeks, chest, and arms.

"I love you," Tulip told him in Akan, which was a first and second language in Ghana.

"I love you too, my beautiful Tulip," Abrafo replied in Akan. He caressed her cheek with the back of his hand and kissed her once more.

Abrafo walked over to the baby's crib sitting across from their bed and against the wall. He looked down into the crib, smiling at his sleeping one-year-old son, Dexter. He was dressed in a royal blue jumper and a pacifier was in his mouth.

"I love you most of all, my little prince," Abrafo told his precious bundle of joy. He kissed his fingertips and touched them to his child's cheek.

***

The elevator chimed before its double doors slid apart and a half dozen killaz poured out. They marched down the hallway behind Abrafo, who was armed with two guns. Every killa accounted for held a shotgun, pistol, or assault rifle. They had them shits out in the open like they had a license to carry them. Two of the killaz were standing on either side of a big black battering ram holding its metal handles. The two-hundred-pound weapon of destruction had 'Big Bad Momma' spray painted on its body and the image of a big, fat, sloppy white woman with long, saggy titties on the head of it. The killaz carrying the battering ram stopped at a gray door with #26 on it. This was the door of Montez's apartment unit.

"Is this the right place?" one of the killaz holding the battering ram asked Abrafo in a whisper. He nodded with assurance and motioned for the rest of the killaz to clear a path. As soon as they did, the ones carrying the battering ram hoisted it up and prepared to slam it into the door.

"Alright, on the count of three we're gonna knock this mothafucka down," the other killa holding the battering ram told the other holding it. He nodded his understanding.

Abrafo frowned, getting the feeling that they were being watched.

"One...two..." the men whispered as they swayed the battering ram forward then backwards, building up momentum to throw all of its two hundred pounds against the door. They stopped their countdown when Abrafo grabbed one of them by the shoulder and looked down the hallway. He looked down the hallway, but he didn't see anyone. Just to be sure, he signaled one of the killaz to check things out. The killa, gripping his shotgun with both hands, cautiously made his way down the corridor, checking around. When he didn't see anyone, he jogged back to where the rest of the crew was and told Abrafo it was clear. Abrafo looked over the hallway once more. He then gave the other killaz the signal to continue with the task of knocking down the door.

"One..." they started their countdown once again.

***

Montez was laid back on his black leather sofa staring up at the rotating ceiling fan while *Dead Presidents* played on the monitor of his 65-inch television set mounted on the wall. His eyes were hooded and snot had run out of his right nostril. A bag of that 'Killuh' dope had him as high as giraffe pussy, and he didn't know when he'd be coming down from it. He had glassy pink eyes and dry tears covering his cheeks. Laid out on the glass coffee table top was his gun, two lines of dope, several packets of Killuh, a Gemstar razor blade, and his cellular.

Montez had never been a man to get high for recreational purposes. He snorted dope to combat his demons. You see, hood movies and street literature novels will have you thinking that the life of a killa was all glamour and glitz. But that couldn't be further from the truth! Ever since the day Montez had caught his first body, he'd been haunted by every life that he'd taken. He was always paranoid and found himself always looking over his shoulders. The poor son of a bitch couldn't shake the feeling that someone was out to get him for some shit he'd done in the past. The thoughts of niggaz coming to take him out like he'd done so many others had him on edge. So much so, that he had to be under the influence in order to deal with everyday life. He also kept a banga on him at all times. It was like his California driver's license.

Montez was sure Assassin was going to send a hit squad at him for his failure to successfully kill KiMani. The reports about the shooting had been all over the news, so he knew Assassin had seen them. On top of that, Assassin, Abrafo, Vato, as well as a couple of the other killaz on Assassin's payroll had blocked him from calling them. Montez understood he was a dead man walking, so he'd planned to get out of town that night.

Montez sat up, digging in his nose. He looked at the slimy, lime-green booger on his pinky finger and wiped it on his jeans. He picked up the half of the plastic straw he'd been using to snort up the dope. Next, he dipped down to the glass coffee table to consume another line. Just when he was about to take some up his left nostril, his cell phone vibrated. He started to ignore it and go on to getting high, but something told him he should answer it.

Montez switched hands with the straw and picked up his cell. He sucked his teeth when he saw it was his nosy ass neighbor, Mrs. Jefferies. Mrs. Jefferies was a 76-year-old lady who'd lost her husband three years ago to natural causes. Since then, she'd elected herself as watch woman of their complex and gathered an obscene amount of cats to act as her guard dogs. The old bird could talk up a storm, but she was as sweet as pecan pie. She'd often bring plates of food for him, and every year for his birthday she'd bake him a chocolate cake and give him a card with twenty dollars in it. Although Montez wasn't in the mood to chit chat, the thought of how nice Mrs. Jefferies was to him made him reconsider ignoring her call. He figured he had twenty minutes he could spare her, so he decided to answer his jack.

"What's up, Mrs. Jefferies? How're you doing?" Montez asked her and dipped low to snort up one of the lines on the glass coffee table. He was about to take it up his left nostril again when she said something that gave him cause for concern.

"Monty, I just seen six men at your door with guns and some big black metal thing," Mrs. Jefferies told him. "I think it's a battering ram or something or other. You best hurry up and get outta there, child. I'm fitsna call the—"

Boom!

Montez's front door came halfway off of its hinges and sent a chunk of the door frame flying. The entire unit seemed to shake like it had been racked by an earthquake. *Boom!* The unit shook again, and the front door crashed down onto the carpet. Instantly, that nigga Montez sobered up and grabbed his piece off the coffee table. He came up on his feet, sending heat at Abrafo and the masked killaz with him.

"Aaaah!" one of them hollered out.

"Gaaah!" another one hollered.

"Raaaah!" a third one hollered and fell to the floor alongside the others.

Seeing Abrafo and the rest of the Killaz upping their guns to lay his ass down, Montez shot at the chain that bound the chandelier to the ceiling. The chain broke and the large chandelier plummeted below. The Killaz looked up at it with terrified eyes, screaming their heads off.

Boom!

The chandelier crashed down on three of the killaz, twisting their limbs in awkward directions and sending blood flying. As blood poured from underneath their dead bodies, Montez ran to the opposite side of his couch and began lifting it up. At this time, Abrafo and the other killaz were getting up from the areas of the floor they'd dove to avoid being crushed by the chandelier. They upped their guns again and started firing at Montez, who was lifting the couch up. Their bullets blew through the couch, tearing holes in it and knocking the stuffing halfway out of it.

With a grunt, Montez pushed the couch forward and the killaz scattered to avoid it. He then turned to the glass sliding door that led to the balcony of his unit. He opened fire on the sliding door, causing breakage in it. Tucking his piece, he ran at the glass door full-speed ahead, with his arms over his face to shield his eyes. Abrafo and the killaz came over the top of the couch, busting on his ass. The combination of their different guns firing sounded like a symphony of bullets.

A line of gunfire trailed behind Montez, shredding up the carpet in his wake. He ran through the sliding door as quickly as he could and busted out the broken glass. Tiny pieces of glass spilled out onto the balcony floor. He was smacked in the face by the icy wind and a light mist of rain. With narrowed eyes, Montez leaped high into the air with his right foot outstretched. His sneaker came upon the guard rail and he pushed up off of it. He flailed his arms and kicked his legs wildly as he plummeted toward the swimming pool below. His hair and shoulders twinkled from the glass on him. Tiny pieces of glass flew up from him from the wind blowing against him. He stared down at the swimming pool, watching its water get closer and closer and closer until he was meeting it.

Splaaash!

The water went high up into the air when Montez broke the surface and nearly reached the bottom of the pool. A burgundy mist came from the two gunshot wounds he'd gotten during his escape. His blood clouded and tainted the water. He could see several bullets zipping straight down in the water and then curving. Then they'd sink to the bottom of the pool.

Goddamn, these niggaz not playing, Montez thought as he swam to the opposite end of the pool, leaving a cloud of blood trailing behind him. *I'ma have to lay low 'til shit cools off and I can get outta town.*

Montez swam up to the surface of the water. He gulped in the air and pulled himself out of the pool. He took off running as fast as he could with a trail of bullets following behind him, but he was lucky enough not to get hit again.

***

"Fuck, we missed 'em!" one of the killaz said to Abrafo. Abrafo nodded and nudged him, pointing to the blood clouding the swimming pool's water.

"Nigga's wounded, so he won't get far. Maybe we can catch 'em," the killa said. At this time, the police cars' sirens were blaring loudly. Mrs. Jefferies had called the cops and they were approaching fast.

Abrafo pulled out a handheld monitor to a tracking device he'd placed on Montez's motorcycle before they came up to his unit. The killa smiled wickedly knowing that they were one step ahead of Montez. Abrafo nudged the killaz and threw his head toward the door for them to follow him out of the unit.

***

Montez huffed and puffed as he made hurried footsteps across the parking lot, leaving wet footprints behind. He held his side and occasionally looked over his shoulder wincing, making sure he wasn't being followed. He wasn't anyone's fool though. He knew that once the kind of killaz that were on him were on you, they wouldn't give up until you were dead. Montez stopped at his lime green and black Kawasaki Ninja 1000. Water dripped from his chin and body as he fished around in his pocket for the key to his bike. He was thankful he hadn't taken it out of his pocket before he'd plopped on the couch to get high.

Montez mounted his motorcycle once he'd found his key. He kicked up its stand, balanced it, and then turned the key in its ignition. As soon as the bike came on, he revved it up louder and louder, then he took off. No sooner than he'd left the parking space he'd parked his Kawasaki Ninja in, Abrafo and the killaz appeared from around the corner of the complex. They upped their guns and started blazing at his ass. Montez ducked his head low and zipped down the parking lot. Bullets flew all around him, but none of them ever hit him. Instead, they pelted the bodies of nearby parked vehicles and shattered some of their windows.

Abrafo pulled out the handheld monitor and looked at its screen. There was a blue blinking dot traveling along the road of a map. The dot represented Montez. Abrafo motioned for the killaz to follow him as he took off running towards the truck they'd taken there. They took off right behind him, determined to catch up with Montez and put his black ass to sleep.

***

"Aye, what's a crackhead's favorite song?" Mack asked with a grin while holding his Heineken.

Hellraiser, who was sharpening his pool stick, glanced back at Lil' Saint. He was sitting on the edge of a neighboring pool table with a Heineken dangling between his legs. His leather jacket was lying beside him. He smirked and shrugged when Hellraiser looked at him. Mack had been hitting them with his corny ass jokes for the greater part of the night.

Hellraiser looked back at Mack. "I know I'm gonna hate myself for this, but fuck it. What?" he inquired and sat the small cubed sharpener on the edge of the pool table.

"I wanna rock right now," Mack told him. He doubled over laughing with his hand on his stomach. He literally had tears forming in his eyes.

"That was just awful," Lil' Saint said and took a swig of his beer.

Hellraiser shook his head and ran his hand down his face. He'd had it with Mack's corny ass jokes. He switched hands with the pool stick, pulled his gun from the small of his back, and pointed it at Mack. "I swear before God, Mack, if you make one more of those dumbass jokes, I'ma shoot chu in yo' mothafucka foot."

"All right, all right, damn, you niggas don't have any sense of humor," Mack said as he wiped away his tears of joy.

"We thought it was funny, daddy," the twins said in unison, and then kissed him on either cheek.

"Thanks, girls," Mack replied with a smile. "Never mind these two uptight negroes. They've got the personalities of a box of fucking rocks." He rolled his head around his shoulders and turned his body from side to side, preparing for his next shot. "Eight ball, right corner pocket!" he called out, tapped the pocket he had in mind with his pool stick, and leaned over the pool table to take the shot. He lined up the tip of his stick with the shiny cue ball and teased it with the intention of hitting it. All eyes were on him as everyone took the occasional swigs of their beer. Julian was in the background pushing a dolly with cases of alcohol into the back room.

Bwap!

The cue ball collided with the eight ball, and the sound resonated throughout the bar. The eight ball slowly rolled across the green, flat surface of the pool table and dropped into the right corner pocket. Mack stood upright, smiling and eyeballing Hellraiser while the twins massaged his shoulders.

"That's game, ol' muscle head-ass nigga," Mack said and took a swig of his Heineken.

Hellraiser pulled out a blue face Benjamin Franklin for their next round of beers. The loser had to pay for their drinks.

"Run it back?" Hellraiser inquired.

"Aye, man, if you don't mind this Cuban heart-throb kicking your ass again, rack 'em up," Mack replied and took another swig of his beer. He sat his beer on the edge of the pool table and passed one of the twins his pool stick. "Gon' head, Blood, I've gotta drain the main vein. All them brews done got to me."

Mack smacked the twins on their asses and startled them. He then made his way towards the men's restroom, singing some song in Spanish.

The telephone started ringing behind the bar while Hellraiser was busy racking the balls on the pool table. He could hear Russell far off in the distance answering the call. The next thing he knew, he was calling him over.

"Yo, Treymaine!" Russell called Hellraiser from across the bar. Hellraiser stood upright and threw his head back like, *What's up?* "You gotta call!"

Hellraiser frowned, wondering who could have been asking to speak to him. His family and friends had the number to his cellphone, so he knew it wasn't anyone close to him.

"Yo, Russ, see who is it?" Hellraiser yelled back across the bar as he picked up his pool stick.

"Nigga, do I look like your secretary? Are you gon' answer this mothafucka or what?" Russell asked him. Hellraiser nodded and laid his pool stick down across the pool table. He saw Russell tell whoever had called for him something before lying the receiver down on the bar top and walking away.

"I'ma knock yo' old ass out one of these days if you keep on talking shit, Russell," Hellraiser told him as they crossed paths. They threw playful punches at each other and Hellraiser patted him on his back good naturedly before walking over to the telephone. "What's up?" he asked as soon as he picked up the jack. He switched hands with it and held it to his ear with his shoulder. He then grabbed a handful of cashews from out of the bowl on the bar top, shook them in his fist, and tossed them back in his mouth. He munched on them as he listened to what he was being told.

"Is this Hellraiser?" the caller asked.

"Yeah, this me, who this though?" Hellraiser fired back.

"This is Nate. You don't know me, homie, but I used to fuck with Hitt-Man real heavy."

Upon hearing Hitt-Man's name mentioned, Hellraiser suddenly stopped munching on the cashews and then grabbed another handful. He started back munching again. "If you rocked with Hitt-Man, then you should know he and I weren't on the best of terms. The mothafucka sent me to prison for fifteen years."

"I know all about that, but I didn't call you to make death threats," Nate assured him. Hellraiser could tell by the way he was talking and then stopping that he was smoking something or other. "Don't get me wrong, I got the heart of a lion and King Kong's nuts, I'm no stranger when it comes to playing with them guns. I don't want no static. At least not with you, I don't."

"Okay, nigga, then what's up? What chu want?" Hellraiser asked curiously. He looked up to Julian rounding the corner. His forehead wrinkled and he threw his head back like, *Who is that?*

"Well, the streets are talking and in my line of business you gotta keep yo' ear to 'em," Nate replied. "The streets saying you looking for the nigga that popped yo' boy and his potna. The man you're looking for just so happens to be an enemy of mine. Are you still there?"

"I'm listening."

Nate went on to spit at Hellraiser what was on his mind. Hellraiser searched behind the bar for an ink pen but he couldn't find one. He looked up at Julian and described what he was looking for with his hand. Julian nodded and looked for an ink pen for him. As soon as he found one, he passed it to Hellraiser who patted him on his shoulder. Next, he grabbed a napkin and wrote down the information Nate was giving him.

"Yeah, I got it," Hellraiser replied as he stared at the information on the napkin. "How do I know I'm not walking into a trap?"

Hellraiser listened as Nate blew out smoke into the air.

"You don't," Nate replied and disconnected the call.

Hellraiser frowned and looked at the receiver. "Rude ass nigga," he said and hung up the telephone.

"Who was that?" Julian asked as he looked over Hellraiser's shoulder at what he'd written down. Hellraiser told him who it was and what he wanted with him.

"If you rolling out to see what's up, be careful, my nigga."

"You know I will," Hellraiser replied and gave him a gangsta hug.

"Alright, you ready for this ass whipping?" Mack asked Hellraiser as he returned from the men's room with his arms hung around the twins' shoulders.

"We'll settle up later. I just gotta lead on the nigga that put the green light on Ki," Hellraiser told him and held up the napkin.

"A lead onna nigga that shot nephew, huh? You need me and mine to roll?" Mack inquired with a serious face. He took his arms from around the twins and walked over to Hellraiser.

"I honestly don't know what type of time this nigga I'm finna go holla at is on. So some back up would be nice," Hellraiser told him. "I mean, if it's not too much trouble."

"What?" Mack asked with a frown and put his hand on Hellraiser's shoulder. "Homeboy, it ain't never too much trouble for me to ride out for you and nephew, we're all family. You fuck with one of us, then you're fucking with all of us. Straight like that."

Hellraiser smirked and gave him a gangsta hug. "I love you, nigga."

"I love you, too," Mack replied and gave him a brotherly pat on the back.

"What's up?" Lil' Saint asked as he walked over, adjusting his eyeglasses. He had his jacket draped over his arm.

Chapter Four

Thunder rumbled and lightning flashed across the dark sky. The rain continued to fall in a mist, slicking the streets wet and making them shine. Mack drove up outside of a two-story house and shifted his whip's gear into park. He, Hellraiser, and Lil' Saint looked out of the window at the house Nate told them to meet him.

"Yo, this the spot?" Mack asked Hellraiser while tapping his semi-automatic gun against his thigh. He wore a bulletproof vest underneath his navy-blue Nike hoodie and his hood hanging just above his brows.

"Yeah, this is it," Hellraiser replied, having made sure the house had the same address Nate had given him. He and Lil' Saint checked the magazines of their guns to make sure them shits were fully loaded. Once they'd confirmed it, they smacked the magazines back into the bottom of their blowers and cocked the slides on them.

Click, clack, click, clack!

Hellraiser and Lil' Saint tucked their guns on their waistlines.

"You sure you can trust this nigga, Blood?" Mack asked, glancing into the backseat at Hellraiser.

"Call me a fool, but for some odd reason, I do," Hellraiser replied, staring out of the window at the two-story house. There were two hittaz standing out on the front porch with their eyes glued on the whip they were in. One of them was wearing a Sacramento Kings fitted cap and the other a Raiders beanie. They were both rocking oversized hoodies. Hellraiser didn't definitely know it, but he was sure they were packing. Why else would they be standing out on the porch when it was cold as fuck, posted up like a couple security guards?

"Is there a reason for that?" Lil' Saint asked over his shoulder.

"The way homie sounded when I was chopping it up with 'em," Hellraiser told him. "He sounded like, how them New York niggaz say, 'dead-ass'? But if dude turns out notta be on the up and up, I swear on the lives of those of my family he gon' be the first to get the business. Straight like that."

"Yo, I'ma park up the block and across the street, in front that yellow house right there," Mack said, pointing out the house he was referring to. Hellraiser and Lil' Saint nodded, letting him know they saw the house he was telling them about. "The twins are parked a ways back inna white van," he told them as he placed an ear bud inside his ear. "Them hoes cocked, locked, and ready to rock if need be. So, if y'all ain't back in say, uh"—he glanced at the time on his cellphone's screen—"fifteen minutes, me and my bitchez running up in there laying shit down."

"My nigga," Hellraiser replied and touched fists with Mack.

Lil' Saint touched fists with him too. Then they hopped out of the car and walked toward the house. The hittaz on the front porch kept a close eye on them while their hands lingered near the bulge on their waistlines.

"Yo, who are you niggaz, fam?" the hitta sporting the baseball cap asked. He was speaking to the other hitta, but his eyes were on Hellraiser and Lil' Saint.

Lil' Saint and Hellraiser waited until they were on the front porch before either of them replied.

"I'm Hellraiser and this the homie Saint." Hellraiser made the introductions. "We're here to holla at Nate. He's expecting us."

"That's cool, but we're gonna have to pat y'all down before y'all go in," the hitta responded and then tapped his man.

His man went to pat Lil' Saint down, and the little man upped his gun. He pointed it right between his eyes and the hitta lifted his hand, surrendering. Before the other hitta could draw his banga, Hellraiser had upped his gun and pressed it to the side of his head.

"I don't think so, young man," Lil' Saint said with a scowl, adjusting his eyeglasses. "Me and my man here are strapped, and I'll be damn if we hand y'all our guns and enter into a den of lions. I was born at night not last night."

"That's right. Y'all heard the man," Hellraiser said with a co-sign, squaring his jaw. If the hitta he had his gun on made the wrong move, he was going to have some extra room inside his fitted cap.

"Yo, it's all good. Nate said to let 'em pass," a nigga with a deep baritone voice said from behind the black-iron screen door.

Lil' Saint and Hellraiser kept their guns on the hittaz a while longer before they eventually lowered them. They tucked them on their waistlines as they headed up the steps with the hittaz mad dogging them along the way. One of the hittaz spat on the front lawn and made threats under his breath, but they didn't pay him any mind. They had bigger fish to fry.

A six-foot-three, olive-complexioned dude opened the front door. He was the nigga with the deep-ass baritone voice. His long hair was in four pigtails, and they were as thick as ropes. He had hazel-green eyes and a six-inch scar that stretched from his forehead, over his eyebrow, and down over his cheek. He was wearing a black T-shirt and the outline of his wife beater could be seen underneath it. He held the front door open with his booted foot while cradling an AR-15 equipped with a scope and infrared laser.

Demetrius, the nigga rocking the pigtails, had a hardened look on his face as Hellraiser and Lil' Saint walked past him into the house. As soon as they crossed the threshold, they were smacked across the face with the overwhelming smell of Kush. It smelled like a knapsack full of dirty assholes. Hellraiser and Lil' Saint heard the door being locked behind them, but they didn't turn around. When they walked inside the living room, there were a total of nine killaz present. They were a bunch of hardcore-looking niggaz bearing tattoos and cradling assault rifles. These gung-ho niggaz looked like extras from the *Menace II Society* movie set.

Hellraiser and Lil' Saint could feel their eyes on them as soon as they walked in. They felt like lambs among a pack of wolves, but they didn't show any fear. They were ready to die inside that living room if need be.

Nate was laid back on the couch with his black Air Forces propped upon the coffee table. A blunt was wedged between his fingers and his AR-15 was lying across his lap. His glassy, red-webbed eyes were focused on the 60-inch flat screen mounted on the wall while his thumbs went back and forth working the PS4 controller. The television's monitor had his undivided attention being that he was in a very intense game of Madden.

Nate was a slim dude, about five-eleven in height with skin the color of a Hershey's kiss. He wore his hair in a fade. It was shaved on the sides but ran deep with waves on the top. A thin mustache complemented his facial features.

Nate seemed to be so wrapped up in his game he neglected the fact he had guests present. It wasn't until Hellraiser cleared his throat with his fist to his mouth that he acknowledged that he and Lil' Saint were there.

"My bad, my nigga, a nigga got caught up in this ol' puss ass game," Nate said, sitting up and pausing the game. He turned off the television with the remote control, tossed it aside, and stood his assault rifle up between his legs. He took a few puffs of his blunt and blew out a cloud of smoke. "What up, my niggaz?" He touched fists with Hellraiser and Lil' Saint and offered them a seat, but they declined to sit down. They wanted to get right to business.

"My man, you said you know where this Assassin kid is at, right? Well, where is he?" Hellraiser asked. "As I'm sure you know, that yee put my son in the 'spital and bodied his best friend. So, you bet cho ass I gotta hard-on for 'em. I want 'em bad, real bad." He balled his fists tight at his sides and his top lip peeled back in a sneer.

"Yeah, I know of a couple of places that lil' bitch be at," Nate assured him while holding smoke in his lungs. He blew out another cloud before continuing what he had to say. "Word is he smoked his pops, and I loved that old nigga like he shot me outta his dick head. He knows I'ma come see 'em, so it's only a matter of time before he comes to see me," he assured him. "I'm thinking yo' killaz and my killaz clique up and we get at this nigga with everything we got. What do you say?"

Hellraiser looked at the floor as he massaged his chin, thinking about the proposal. His crew was small, but they were about that gangsta shit. The way he looked at it, if he had an entire army of cold killa niggaz at his disposal, they could squash Assassin and his old faggot-ass crew. Hellraiser lifted his head and his hand, slapping five with Nate and then gripping his fingers—that universal greeting that all brothers gave each other when they linked up.

A smiling Nate nodded. "That's what I'm talking 'bout, big dog, we're on this nigga."

Hellraiser cracked a smirk as he replied, "Let's do it then." He dapped up Nate.

The living room went wild with the killaz hollering and cheering while holding their assault rifles in the air. Nate, holding his AR-15 in one hand, signaled for them to quiet down with the hand he held his blunt in.

"Yo, so where does this brotha primarily be?" Lil' Saint inquired with a serious expression across his face.

"Shiiiit, knowing him, there's only one of three places he would be. And that's the—" Nate was cut short by his cellphone ringing and vibrating in his pocket. He held up a finger for Lil' Saint to give him a minute, then he pulled it out. He wasn't familiar with the number hitting him up, but he decided to answer it anyway.

"What up?" Nate spoke into his jack, blowing smoke up at the ceiling.

"What up, you ol' certified bitch made-ass nigga?" Vato replied.

Nate stopped the blunt at his lips, hearing the familiar voice. His heart started racing and he frowned. The expression on his face made everyone in the room exchange glances, then they looked back at him. They wondered what was wrong. Hellraiser threw his head back like, *What's up?* And Nate replied by throwing up his hand for him to leave him alone.

"If it isn't ol' ho-ass Vato, Assassin's young fucking flunky! I don't know how you got the number to my jack, but I'm glad you called," Nate said after regaining his composure and continuing to smoke his blunt. "'Cause I want to let chu know personally that me and my niggaz gon' squash you and that puss ass boss of yours."

"Oh, yeah? That's yo' word?"

Nate took the time to blow out smoke and mash his blunt out in the ashtray before replying. "Yeah, nigga, that's my word!"

A red dot appeared on Nate's forehead—*Pewk!* A bullet zipped right through the living room window, leaving a hole the size of a nickel in Nate's forehead and erupting out the back of his skull. His blood misted the air and he fell backward to his death, dropping his AR-15. Instantly, Demetrius and the other killaz upped their assault rifles to defend themselves. As soon as they did, a line of rapid gunfire cut through the living room window, shattering its glass chaotically. One after another, the killaz collapsed to the floor, leaving their misty blood freefalling.

"Aaaaah!"

"Aaaaah!"

The hittaz screamed one after the other as they were cut down by automatic gunfire. Right after, there was hushed talking among a few men as they charged the steps of the house. Their booted feet resonated inside of the house as they flooded the front porch.

"Y'all niggaz fallback, I'm 'bouta kick this bitch down!" one of the masked killaz told the others.

Boom, boom!

The front door rattled from brute force as the masked killa tried to kick it down. Hellraiser, who was squatted low behind the couch, with Lil' Saint by his side, looked from the front door to the windows alongside the house. He could hear the killaz running towards the backyard. That meant that they were coming through the backdoor. They were going to box them in and slaughter them!

"Fuck! Saint, help me push this couch against the front door," Hellraiser told him and tucked his gun. Lil' Saint tucked his too. Together, they hoisted the couch from the floor and brought it to the front door, leaning it against it. "Come on! We've gotta barricade the backdoor." Hellraiser motioned for him to follow him to the kitchen as he took off running.

Shatter! Froosh! Shatter! Froosh!

Molotov cocktails burst through the window alongside the house. They exploded on the living room floor, and fire swept throughout the house creating the Devil's lair. There was more shattering and explosions of fires as more Molotov cocktails were hurled through the living room window. They exploded when they collided with the floor, adding more fire to what was already there.

Hellraiser and Lil' Saint narrowly missed the flying Molotov cocktails as they exploded mere inches away from their sneakers. They disappeared into the kitchen. Lil' Saint yanked the refrigerator's cord out of the wall and then ran to the side of it that Hellraiser was on. Together, they grunted while pushing the big Frigidaire across the floor towards the backdoor. The backdoor was rattling with loud bangs coming from it. The backdoor was threatening to burst loose from its hinges. In fact, the mothafucka did, right when Hellraiser and Lil' Saint had pushed the refrigerator over. It made a loud sound—*Boom!*—falling directly in front of the backdoor and stopping the killaz from entering.

"This mothafucka not coming open!" Hellraiser and Lil' Saint overheard one of the killaz tell another.

"We gon' blast this bitch apart then! Y'all niggaz stand back!" Vato, who was leading the charge, told the killa.

The window over the kitchen sink shattered, and two more Molotov cocktails flew through it. They exploded upon impact and fire spread throughout the kitchen. Hellraiser and Lil' Saint barely managed to duck the bottles.

"Come on, Saint!" Hellraiser nudged him and took off back towards the living room.

Buratatatataatat, buratatatatat, ratatatatatat!

Automatic gunfire Swiss cheesed the backdoor. Vato kicked some of the broken wood inward and used the stock of his assault rifle to knock the rest of it in. He leaped on top of the refrigerator, to the floor, and then took off after Hellraiser and Lil' Saint. He motioned for the killaz to follow him with his assault rifle as he gave chase.

Ba-Boom!

The front door flew open and knocked the couch to the floor as Hellraiser and Lil' Saint were headed toward the staircase. They were halfway up the steps when the masked killaz poured in from the kitchen and the living room. Hellraiser was the first to reach the upper level, so he pulled out his gun and laid some cover fire down for Lil' Saint.

Bocka, bocka, bocka, bocka!

Hellraiser's tool slightly jumped as it spat fire at his opps. He winded up striking two of them down. One went tumbling back down the staircase from a fatal head wound while the other caught three in his bulletproof vest. He slid to the side down the wall, leaving a smear of blood in his wake. One of the three bullets had gone straight through his body armor and out of his back. His face was balled up in agony, but he actually looked like he was in the middle of taking a shit.

Hellraiser motioned for Lil' Saint to go into the master bedroom while he held him down. He continued to get busy with the charging killaz until his gun clicked empty. He didn't realize he'd spent every bullet he had left, so he looked at his blower like it was defective. Right then, Vato and the rest of the killaz was upping their automatic weapons.

"Oh, fuck!" Hellraiser shouted, and his eyes bulged fearfully. He dove out of the way as rapid gunfire came in angry bursts. Hole after hole appeared along the staircase's wall and sent debris into the air.

Hellraiser barely managed to escape without getting his head blown off, so he was thankful he'd gotten away. He came up from the floor fast, running inside of the master bedroom and slamming the door shut. His face was sweaty and sticky from the high temperature of the raging fire, and he was breathing hard as hell. He locked the door behind him, reloaded his gun, and motioned Lil' Saint over from the window where he was busy raising it.

Lil' Saint darted over to Hellraiser and helped him push the nightstand across the bedroom door. No sooner than they finished moving the nightstand where they wanted it, the front door started rattling again. The killaz were trying to kick that bitch down and murder them.

"Through the window, I've gotta plan!" Lil' Saint motioned for Hellraiser to follow him, and he did. Once Lil' Saint was out of the window, he grabbed Hellraiser's hand and pulled him out. Hellraiser followed him up to the top of the house. Hunched down, they could see more big black Suburban trucks pulling up among the other three that were already there. The doors of the SUVs were popping open, and armed killaz were hopping out. They were storming the house like World War II soldiers or some shit.

"Goddamn, this nigga not playing, it looks like half the fucking city after us," Hellraiser said, taking all the killaz in from a bird's eye view. Lil' Saint was standing beside him removing his black leather belt. Hellraiser followed suit and wrapped his leather belt around his knuckle. "What's up, Saint?"

"We're gonna use these power lines to glide over to the other side," Lil' Saint told him and pointed over to the opposite house.

Hellraiser's forehead crinkled, thinking of getting the shit shocked out of him from touching one of the power lines. "I don't know, Saint, wouldn't touching one of those lines electrocute us?"

"Nah, birds can sit on power lines and not get electrocuted 'cause they're so far up from the ground," Lil' Saint explained. "All we've gotta do is stay away from the ground or anything in contact with it and the electricity will stay in the power line."

"You sure about this?"

"Yep, the lines are already wet from the rain, so we shouldn't have any problem getting over there. I'll go first."

Lil' Saint ran as fast as he could and leaped high across the air. He came off the rooftop of the house, grabbed the outstretched line, swung his belt over the top of it and grasped it firmly. He held the belt tightly as he quickly glided to the other side of the street. Hellraiser, holding his hand above his brows, smiled as he watched him disappear into the darkness before his eyes.

"It worked, it actually fucking worked," a smiling Hellraiser said to no one particular. Hearing something at his back, just that fast, his face balled in hostility and he went on the defense. In one swift motion, he whipped around, pulled his gun, and came up with it spitting hot shit. His gun slightly jumped in his hand as it cut down Vato and one other killa coming up the rooftop with their assault rifles.

"Aaaaah!"
"Aaaaah!"

Vato and the masked killa went down one after the other. Their assault rifles went up in the air as they collided with the rooftop and went sliding downward. They were still screaming in freefall. Their voices got smaller and smaller until Hellraiser heard two thuds below. Seeing more killaz coming out the window, Hellraiser knew it was time he got his ass up out of there. He tucked his gun in the small of his back and took off running in what looked like slow motion. As he got airborne, the killaz came out of the window of the master bedroom clutching their assault rifles with both hands. There were also masked killaz that had just spilled back out of the burning house. The first one to make it out on the lawn, motioned the other ones over and pointed up at Hellraiser. The killaz came together in a crowd and upped their assault rifles at Hellraiser.

Hellraiser grasped the power line, swung the end of his belt over it and held it firmly. As soon as he had a firm grip on the belt, he rocketed towards the opposite side of the street. Time seemed to speed back up then! And the sounds of automatic gunfire resonated throughout the night, coming from the rooftop behind Hellraiser and the grounds below. The bullets zipped up, down, and all around him, but through the grace of God Almighty, he went unscathed.

Skirrrrrt!

A van lurched forward as it halted sideways in the middle of the residential block. Both of its doors popped open, and the twins hopped out. They wore ski masks over their faces, bulletproof vests on their bodies, and clutched M-16 assault rifles. They ran up on the front lawn of the burning house and upped their rifles.

Buratatatatatatatat!
Buratatatatatatatat!

Fire spat out of the twins' M-16s, chopping the masked killaz down. They made blood-curdling screams as they plummeted toward the ground. As a few of them lay on the lawn barely alive, the girls put a few more bullets into their bodies to finish them off.

A few masked killaz ran from the side of the house blazing at the twins. A few of their bullets struck the twins' van and even the windshield.

One twin stood in front of the other to lay down some cover fire while the other reloaded her assault rifle. As soon as she cocked her shit, she upped it and started spitting at the opposition. The masked killaz hollered one after the next as they were taken off their feet.

"I'ma go get the van, hold me down!" the twin told her sister. Her sister nodded, and she ran back to the van and hopped in. She honked the horn and her sister fled from the gunfight with two remaining masked killaz chasing after her. Once she'd jumped into the van and slammed the door shut, the van sped away. The two masked killaz ran out into the middle of the street firing at them.

Man, the twins saved my ass, good looking, girls, Hellraiser thought. *Where the hell did Mack go?*

Hellraiser's brows furrowed, wondering where Mack's ass had gone. When he looked down, he saw Lil' Saint staring up at him from an alley. The alley was behind a house with a pool he was sure he'd landed in when he had glided over. The little man was standing right beside Mack's whip, so he figured he'd hit him up to pick them up. Lil' Saint pointed at the house that Hellraiser was sliding towards on the line. Hellraiser looked back and forth between his friend and the house. That's when he realized he was directing him to drop inside of the pool. He further understood this when Lil' Saint waved his hand up and down, signaling for him to let go of the line.

"Okay, here goes nothing," Hellraiser said as he released the other end of his belt. He plummeted towards the pool below him. It appeared to be coming up at him faster and faster and before he knew it—*Splash!* Water went high up into the air and shortly after, Hellraiser came back up drenched. He came out of the pool dripping and clutching his gun. He heard footsteps approaching him from behind and could see some of the killaz coming at him through the small openings of the wooden fence.

A whistle rang out in the night, and he looked in front of him. Lil' Saint was sitting on top of the gate that separated the house from the alley, with an M-16 assault rifle equipped with a scope. He switched gloved hands with the deadly firearm and motioned for Hellraiser.

"I got cho back, homeboy," Lil' Saint assured him as he upped his M-16 and looked through the scope. Hellraiser tucked his gun at the small of his back and began climbing the fence.

Lil' Saint watched the masked killaz as they began to climb the fence. One of them was halfway over the fence while the other had grabbed it and threw his booted foot over. Lil' Saint relaxed his breathing and lined the crosshairs of his rifle up with the first one's forehead. He pulled the trigger, the bullet whispered from the muzzle, and zipped through the air. It zeroed in on the masked killa's forehead like a heat-seeking missile. The masked killa looked up in a nick of time for his forehead to be obliterated. His blood and brain particles misted the air, and he fell back over the fence. The other masked killa's eyes bulged, seeing his comrade get his wig split. He looked in Lil' Saint's direction and went to jump down, but it was already too late.

Lil' Saint's next bullet zipped through the air, like a bumble bee, in route to the last masked killa's forehead—*Splaaaatttt!* The impact of the slug launched the masked killa's head to the left along with a mist of blood that slowly fell to the ground. He did a back flip off the fence and smacked down against the pavement.

"Yeah, I still got it," Lil' Saint said as he lowered his M-16. He switched hands with the assault rifle and helped Hellraiser over the fence. They both jumped down to the gravelly ground in the alley and darted to the getaway car. They hopped in, slammed their doors, and the whip sped away, leaving dirt clouds in its wake.

Chapter Five

"Fuck, fuck, fuck!" Hellraiser shouted as he pounded his fist against the dashboard.

"What's up? What happened back there?" Mack asked as he adjusted the rearview mirror and looked up at it. He could see the anger plastered across Hellraiser's face.

"Homeboy was looking to clique up and smash this fool Assassin," Hellraiser told him and slammed his fist into his palm for emphasis.

"That nigga Nate you were telling me about?" Mack asked him. Lil' Saint was riding shotgun, fogging his eyeglasses and cleaning them with a handkerchief.

"Yeah, that nigga, man, he was just about to tell us where ol' boy be at when a sniper knocked 'em down. Next thing me and Saint know, a million hittaz rush the spot chopping shit down. Fuck!" Hellraiser shouted, slamming his fists down on the seat beside him. He then clenched his jaws so tight that the vein at his temple twitched angrily. Hellraiser's cellular rang beside him and stole his attention. He recalled leaving it there on the backseat before he and Lil' Saint went to holla at that nigga Nate.

"Who hitting you up?" Lil' Saint asked, sliding his eyeglasses back on.

"Julian. I hope this nigga ain't 'bouta hit me with some more bad news," Hellraiser said, looking at his cellphone's screen. He answered the call and placed the cellular to his ear. "What up?"

***

"Yo, Russell," Julian called out to his employee as he cleaned the glasses and placed them where they were supposed to be. Russell, who was sitting in the chairs on top of a table, looked to him and threw his head back like, *What's up?* "Do me a favor, shut and lock the door. I don't want any stragglers stumbling in here," he told him, toothpick bobbing up and down.

Russell, a six-foot, caramel-skinned man with a graying goat-ee, held up a thumb and made his way over to the front door entrance of the establishment. As he walked off to do like he'd been asked, Julian began rapping "Flashlight" softly while untying the black apron from around his waist.

"Uhhh, Julian," Russell called out to his boss with a panic-stricken voice. When Julian looked, he was wide eyed and his mouth was hanging open. A gun was pressed to his forehead and he was slowly taking steps back. The man behind the trigger was Montez. He was pale as fuck and sweating profusely while holding his side. Julian didn't know what to think of him, but he got a hell of a lot of bad vibes from him.

Well, fuck me doggy style, this is the exact reason why I told this nigga to lock the goddamn door, Julian thought as he shook his head. *If it wasn't some fucking drunk that stumbled in here, I knew it would be some fucking crackhead looking to stick the place up for his next fix.*

Keeping his eyes on Russell, who was holding his hands up in the air surrendering, Montez reached back to lock the door behind him.

"Keep your hands were I can see 'em, old man, or I'll put your fucking brains on the ceiling," Montez warned with an angry expression. He was looking ill as shit, but he was still as danger-ous as he ever was. Therefore, he meant what he told Russell. "As a matter of fact, old head, say ah."

"Ah—goomp!" Russell sounded like he'd swallowed some-thing when Montez shoved his gun in his grill.

"Youngsta, there's no need for things to get bloody," Julian told him with his hands held up. "I gotta 'bout five hunnit dollars on me and whatever's inside the register you can have," he assured him. "All I ask is you let ol' Russ there live. Man's gotta wife, four children, and six grandchildren."

"I don't want your money, Julian," Montez told him without looking his way. The gunman knowing him on a first-name basis surprised the shit out of him. His crinkled brows made this obvious.

"How do you know my name, young bruh?" Julian asked. Julian ran his face through his mental database, but he didn't come up with anything. He was sure he didn't know him.

"You'd be surprised what you can find out about your enemies and their friends when you shove a gun in the right faces," Montez replied. He was wincing every time he talked due to his wounds.

Julian was frowned up now. He knew the young nigga had to be the opps. "The pieces of the puzzle are starting to come together now. You're Hitt-Man and Assassin's people...you've come here to take me out?" His eyes darted to the nickel-plated shotgun sitting behind the bar. If he could get his hands on it, he and Russell had a chance at living to see another day.

"Wrong again, OG," Montez said. Julian was confused now. He angled his head and looked at him crazily. "Me and Assassin's people are beefing on the account that I botched the hit on Hellraiser's boy, KiMani. Now that lil' shit and that bitch have sicced their goons on me," he told him. "They've been chasing me all over the city and there's no place to hide. Nowhere is safe for me!"

"I guess you want me to feel sorry for you after you tried to kill my nephew? Well, God forgives but I don't, nigga," Julian told him. "But I tell you what, you tell me that sob story again and I'll break out with the violin and play some sad music over it."

"I didn't come here looking for sympathy," Montez shot back. "I came here to make a deal."

"What kinda deal?" Julian asked.

"One I'm sure ya man won't say no to."

"I'm listening."

"You put me up 'til I can recover and leave town, and I'll give you yo' boy."

"You got it."

"Nah." Montez shook his head no. "Your word doesn't mean jack shit to me. I want chu to get cha man Hellraiser on the phone. I hear he's a man of his word," he told him. "If he gives me his word that y'all a put me up 'til I'm good, then I'll serve you

Assassin's ass onna silver platter, roasted with a fucking apple in his mouth."

"I'ma needa to make that call."

"I'm not gonna stop ya."

Julian placed his Bluetooth on his ear and picked up his cellular. He hit up Hellraiser. His cellphone rang twice before he picked it up. Julian told him what was up and he agreed to the proposition Montez presented.

"Yo, my man says he's with it," Julian informed him.

"Put that shit on speaker. I needa hear it come from the horse's mouth," Montez replied.

Julian told Hellraiser to say it again after he'd put his jack on speakerphone. "What's yo' name, homie?" Hellraiser asked.

"Montez."

"Well, Montez, you shoot my man Julian the address and draw us up a blueprint of this Assassin's crib, how many killaz he keeps on deck, and you've gotta deal," Hellraiser said loud and clear over the speakerphone.

"I can do that. No problem," Montez assured him. "But I'm not coming off that info until I recover. Once a nigga done healed up, you'll get all you need to squash this fool."

"No can do, bruh. I need the info first."

"How do I know you're not gonna pop my ass once I give you what you want?"

"My man said you know me to be a man of my word, is that true?"

"Yeah."

"Well, right now, I'm giving you my word as a man that I will not harm a hair on yo' head as long as you gemme the info I want," Hellraiser told him. "Do we have ourselves a deal?"

"We've gotta deal."

"Good," Hellraiser replied. "Now will you do me a favor and take that pistol outta Russell's mouth?"

"Sure. No problem." Montez took his gun out of Russell's mouth. He saw it was glistening with his saliva, so he wiped it on his button-down shirt.

"Thanks, uhhhh, what's your name again, homie?"

"Montez. But you can call me Tez."

"Ok. Cool," Hellraiser replied. "Look here, sit tight. I'll be there inna minute."

"All right," Montez said as he took a chair from off one of the tables and sat down. He was still uneasy about the entire situation, so he held tight to his gun and kept his eyes on the older men present.

"Yo, Julian, do me a favor and pour my boy Tez a drink," Hellraiser told him. "Whatever he has is on me, put it on my tab. Then I'd like for you to give that doctor friend of ours a call so he can come check 'em out. You think you can do that for me?"

"Yeah, Blood, I've got chu covered," Julian said.

"Appreciate chu, bruh." Hellraiser disconnected the call.

"What would you like to drink, Tez?" Julian asked him with both his hands on the bar top.

"I'd like an, uh, double shotta Evan Williams," Montez replied, wincing and holding his side.

"Double shotta E-Dub coming up," Julian said, pulling out a glass and then taking out the bottle of Evan Williams with the jigger nozzle. He poured the requested amount of liquor and was about to put the bottle away when Montez said something else to him.

"Nah, bring me the bottle, man," Montez told him as he balled up his face in agony and leaned to the side. He pulled some of the bloody duct tape down and took a look at the wounds he sustained during a shootout with Assassin's goons. The holes in him looked like they were still running with blood.

"Lemme take a look," Julian said, sitting the glass and bottle on the table top. He kneeled down and held back the duct tape. He frowned seeing Montez's bloody wounds. "Yeah, this looks bad. You're gonna fuck around and bleed to death if you don't get some medical attention fast," he warned him. When he looked up at him, he was finishing the glass of liquor he'd brought him and then removing the jigger out of the bottle. He poured some of the alcohol on his wounds, which felt like salt to them. He squeezed his eyes shut and growled from the sensational burning he endured. Afterwards, he took the bottle to his head and guzzled the liquor. It felt like a flaming river pouring down his throat and coating his belly. "Aaaah!" he hissed from the strong bourbon burning his mouth, and wiped his wet chin.

"Great. How soon can you get here?" Julian asked the doctor over his Bluetooth. He'd already picked up a notepad, now he was searching behind the bar for an ink pen. This entire time, Russell was sitting the chairs on the table top and mad dogging Montez. He didn't like the fact he'd stuck a gun in grill. It hurt his ego and made him feel like a bitch. Had it not been for Hellraiser needing him to track down the nigga that ordered his son killed, then he would have shot his bitch ass.

"Here you go." Julian sat down the ink pen and notepad in front of Montez. "Oh, no, I'm talking to a patron," he told the good doctor. "Ok. I'll see you then." He disconnected the call. He looked back and forth between the mad dog stares of Montez and Russell. They looked like they were about ready to have a shootout. Montez was gripping his gun tightly and Russell had his hand near his holstered piece.

"I feel heat coming from over there, OG, you got something on yo' mind?" Montez asked. His sweaty, pale face made him look like he had a fever, but should Russell want to try his hand at a game of chance, he'd oblige him.

"Yeah, I got it on my mind to putta bullet in yo' punk ass, bitch," Russell said angrily, clenching and unclenching his jaws, hand on the handle of his gun.

Montez's eyebrows slanted and his nostrils flared. His gun was aimed directly at Russell's hostile ass. "Hey, if you see a bitch then shoota bitch." He smiled wickedly. Julian frowned, peeping what was about to go down between the two men. He knew he had to stop things before they got out of control.

"Yo, y'all knock this shit off right now," Julian said, stepping between the two men, putting himself in the line of fire. "Y'all not gon' sit up here and shoot my shit up. I runna respectable business here. If you two cowboys wanna have a showdown, then I suggest you do it after we settle our business. Do I make myself clear?" He looked back and forth between them. Montez nodded. It took Russell a while but he conceded as well. "Good. Now put your pieces away." They obliged his command.

Julian sat down at the table with Montez as he wrote down the address to Hitt-Man's mansion, where Assassin and Niqua were holed up. He drew up a blueprint of the place as well, showing him the ins and outs of the estate, as well as the hittaz he had guarding the place. When Montez had finished going over the details of the blueprint with Julian, there were bloody fingerprints and smears of blood on the notepad's paper.

Julian tore the sheet of paper from the notepad, folded it, and slid it into his pocket. He grabbed Montez under his arm and helped him to his feet. "Come on. There's a bedroom made up in the back where I keep the inventory. I'll keep you housed there until this entire thing blows over," he told him. "The doc should be here in say, uh," he glanced at his timepiece, "10 or 15 more minutes."

"Okay. Ughh!" Montez replied, hollering in pain from his wounds. He grabbed the bottle of Evan Williams from the table top and made his way alongside Julian to the back of the bar.

"Russ, I'm finna take youngin' to the back, keep an ear open for the doc," Julian called out to him. Russell, who was now sweeping the floor, nodded understandingly and went back to his duty.

Booooom!

A black Chevrolet Suburban with a crash bar plowed through the entrance of Bottoms Up like a wrecking ball. The impact sent the broken doors and chunks of walls spilling onto the floor of the bar. The Chevy's doors popped open. Mad goons wearing ski masks and dressed in all black hopped out. Their eyes twinkled with murder, their jaws were squared, and their gloved hands were gripping Dracos equipped with infrared lasers and drums.

Within seconds, the goons were crawling over the establishment like cockroaches on some search and destroy shit.

"Oh, shit!" Julian's eyes got big seeing what was going down.

"They musta followed me here!" Montez shouted to Julian, casting his bottle of liquor aside and upping his gun. He started taking cover, blasting at the opposition while Julian duck and ran behind the bar to get to his nickel-plated shotgun. The bottles of liquor lined up on the shelves behind the bar exploded in broken glass and alcohol. Julian dove to the ground and pulled out his shotgun. It was already locked and loaded. He pulled a belt lined with shells for the weapon from out of its hiding place behind the bar and looped it over his head. He squeezed his eyes shut and gritted his teeth. More bottles exploded and more liquor and broken glass rained down on him.

"Fuck this shit, Blood!" Julian spat heatedly. He felt like a bitch being on the losing end of a gun battle and wanted to turn the tables. Heart thumping and adrenaline flowing fast and hard throughout his veins, he sprung up from the floor. He made his way to the opposite side of the bar with his shotgun spitting flames at the masked gunmen.

Bloom, bloom, bloom, bloom!

Howls of pain filled the air as some of the gunmen were struck down while others were instantly killed by headshots. Julian ducked back down behind the bar and made his way over to the end of it. His forehead was peppered with beads of sweat and he was breathing heavily. The last thing he saw before ducking back down for cover were the goons closing in on Russell. Russell was moving strategically around the pool tables, taking the occasional shot at them. Although he was armed like Julian and Montez, his gun didn't really stand a chance against their automatic weapons.

"Psst, psst!" Montez called for Julian's attention. When Julian looked, he saw him hidden within the doorway of the backdoor exit. He was holding his gun at his side. He looked to be doing worse than when he'd come to the bar earlier that night. His face had gotten paler and he was dripping blood on the floor. Julian figured it must have been due to the fact his adrenaline was pumping from the gun battle, which produced a faster flow of blood.

Montez, through hand signals, told him that there were a total of twelve goons on deck and they'd taken out four altogether. Julian nodded to let him know he understood, then he stole a peek from around the corner of the bar. Russell was hunched down and holding his side. His pained facial expressions let Julian know he'd been shot and from the looks of things, his life was coming to a close. Russell was doing as he was the last time he saw him, taking covering behind the pool tables and taking shots at the masked goons. He'd managed to strike a couple of them, but those sons of bitchez were wearing body armor, which saved them from a bloody death.

Splocka, splocka, splocka, splocka!

Russell popped up for a split second and sent fire at the goons coming for his head. Unfortunately, he didn't hit any of them and his gun was clicking empty every time he pulled its trigger. He threw the useless gun aside and snatched one of the pool sticks from off the table. He crossed himself in the sign of the Holy crucifix, realizing he was in his final minutes of life. Next, he broke the pool stick over his knee and created two spears.

Fuck, Russell! I gotta do something to even the odds here, Julian thought, looking around for something that would give them a fighting chance. His eyes came across a few bottles of alcohol and white rags. He smirked, thinking how they'd make great Molotov cocktails.

Julian told Montez his plan and for him to lay down some cover fire for him when he gave him the signal. Still wincing, Montez nodded in agreement. Shortly, he got to work making up the Molotov cocktails, creating a total of four and lighting the ends of their rags.

"Come on, you sons of bitchez, let's dance!" Russell hollered like he was charging into battle. Julian's eyes widened hearing his dear friend hollering the way he was. His heart dropped to the pit of his stomach and his eyes turned glassy, fearing the worse.

Julian sat down his shotgun and picked up two of the Molotov cocktails. He peeked around the corner of the bar to see Russell, on top of a pool table, swinging the broken pool sticks. He struck a couple of the masked gunmen across their faces and kicked one in the chest. He flew across the room, landing awkwardly on his back at the edge of the pool table, and then fell on his stomach on the floor. His victory was short lived as the rest of the goons rushed forward and painted his ass red. Old Russell looked like he'd been struck with a barrage of rotten tomatoes from his head down to his feet. He stayed still for a second, bleeding and smoking, but finally fell to the floor.

Julian's bulging eyes saw Russell fall to his bloody death in slow motion, four times. His eyes instantly became watery and his bottom lip trembled. He ignored his plan with Montez and started launching the Molotov cocktails at the opps.

"You mothafuckaaaaaaz!" Julian screamed, teary eyed, watching the flaming bottles hurl across the room.

Boom! Froosh! Boom! Froosh! Boom! Froosh! Boom! Froosh!

"Aaaaaaah!" one of the goons screamed as he was engulfed in flames.

"Raaaaaah!" a second goon screamed as he was set on fire.

"Gaaaaaah!" a third goon screamed as fire swept up his body.

Tears streamed down an angry Julian's cheeks as he upped his shotgun and started busting at the masked men. Montez came behind him, letting niggaz have it with his gun. They took out the burning goons as they fired their assault rifles recklessly. Some of them bumped into their comrades and accidentally set them ablaze as well. They hollered out in agony but were quickly slumped by Julian and Montez. Once the last of them had fallen, Julian and Montez scanned the bar while reloading their weapons. The golden fires illuminated their faces as they fed their guns and cocked the slides on them. Suddenly, the lights flickered out and the backdoor rumbled like an angered ram was smashing into it repeatedly.

Julian and Montez whipped around to the back exit door. It was dark, but thanks to the fires behind them, they were able to make out some things. Julian looked to Montez and saw that more and more blood was splashing at his foot. He didn't know how long he'd be standing beside him, but he hoped it would be long enough to fend off the predators trying to get in.

"You good, youngin'?" Julian asked, wiping the sweat from his forehead.

Montez nodded yes, but he knew better.

Boom! Boom! Ba-boom!

The backdoor burst open and masked goons flooded the opposite side of the bar. Julian and Montez upped their guns and started blasting, laying niggaz the fuck out.

"Hold it down. I needa reload!" Julian shouted to Montez. He kneeled down, held his shotgun at his side upside down, and began feeding its belly with shells. Montez, holding his wound, continued to fire at the masked killaz as they spilled inside the bar. As soon as he dropped the one in front of him, Abrafo appeared with his big ass bowie knife with the spiked fist guard. In a three swift motions, he sliced off the hand Montez was using to hold his gun, sliced his throat with his spiked fist guard, and slammed his knife into his chest. Montez's eyes bulged and his mouth quivered, with blood overflowing his chin. Abrafo lifted him incredibly high into the air. His arms and feet dangled in mid-air while his blood pelted the floor. His eyes blinked and watered while his mouth continued to quiver and spill blood.

Julian had just finished reloading and cocking his shotgun. He looked beside him and saw blood splashing on the floor. His brows crinkled. He looked upward to see Montez dangling from the end of Abrafo's knife. He suddenly went still, and that's when Julian knew he was dead.

Sniiiikt!

Abrafo snatched his bowie knife out of Montez's chest, and he fell to the floor with a thud. Julian had just pointed his shotgun at him when the killa sliced it in half and rendered it useless. A surprised expression came across Julian's face as he examined both halves of his shotgun. He threw the halves to the floor, rolled his head around his shoulders, and threw his fists up. He was ready for a fight now.

"Come on! Come on, you big bitch!" Julian said, dancing around him and throwing phantom punches and jabs. "Throw down the knife and let's see how you get it from the shoulders."

Abrafo wiped his bloody knife on his pants and sheathed it where he'd pulled it from. He whistled sharply and motioned forward with his gloved hand. A second later, a handful of masked goons spilled in from the hole in the wall as well as the backdoor. They surrounded Julian and pumped hot bullets into him, spinning him around like a ballerina wearing ice skates. Once they stopped firing, their Dracos smoked and a moment later, Julian, who was bloody and bleeding at the mouth, crashed to the floor. The illumination from the fires scattered throughout the floor shined on his face and body. Abrafo and the goons watched him for a minute, and then they vanished like a clan of ninjas.

A few minutes later, Hellraiser, Lil' Saint, Mack, and the twins entered the bar with guns at their sides. Their heads were on swivels as they looked around at all of the damage and dead bodies covering the floor. When Hellraiser laid eyes on Russell, it saddened him, but when he saw how niggaz had done Julian, it broke his heart in two.

"Aww, nah, not my nigga!" Hellraiser said with a hurt-filled voice. He and the others rushed over to Julian. He was bleeding badly and there were an awful amount of holes in him. Kneeling, Hellraiser sat his gun down on the floor beside him and turned Julian over onto his back. Just then, the doctor that Julian had called, Doctor Jaelyn CarMichael, stepped inside of the establishment one foot at a time, holding a black leather bag in his hand and adjusting his wire-framed eyeglasses.

"Jesus Christ," Doctor CarMichael said, taking in the dead men lying about. When he saw who Hellraiser was holding in his arms, he shut his eyes and shook his head. He then crossed himself in the sign of the Holy Crucifix.

"Damn, my nigga, Julian." Hellraiser shook his head as tears burst from his eyes and slicked his cheeks wet. "Fuck, man, you weren't supposed to go out like this. Any other way, but not like this."

"Ugh!" Julian moaned in agony, surprising Hellraiser. He quickly wiped away his tears and looked him in the eyes. He could see he was trying to say something, but it was hard for him to get it out. As he struggled to say what was on his mind, he coughed up blood. What looked like pasty tomato sauce oozed out either side of his mouth and dripped on the floor. "Check—check—c—check—my—my pocket."

"O—okay, man," Hellraiser told him as he checked his pockets. "I'ma check yo' pockets. But you—you stay with m—me, okay?" Julian didn't say shit. He lay in his homie's arms, bleeding like a stuck pig. Hellraiser didn't find anything in Julian's pocket besides a wad of money and a pack of opened Spearmint gum. It wasn't until he went inside of his other pocket that he found the folded sheet of paper Montez had written Hitt-Man's address and the blueprints to his mansion on. He showed Julian what he'd found in his pocket: "Is this it, Julian? Is this what chu wanted me to have?" Julian nodded as more blood oozed out of his grill. His eyes then rolled to the back of his head, and his body went limp. "No, no, no, no! Don't do this, man! Don't chu do this to us! We need you, Julian. Da Crew needs you, man." Hellraiser broke down sobbing with snot bubbling out of his nose. He hugged Julian to him as he wept. When he heard police car sirens drawing near him, he knew it was time for him to go, so he lay Julian down against the floor. He then closed his eyes and kissed him gently on the forehead. "I love you, bruh. We all do. We'll see you when we get there. Just be sure to save us all a place." He wiped his wet eyes and sniffled.

Tranay Adams

Chapter Six

Vato was thankful he'd worn a bulletproof vest when Hellraiser had blasted on him. Otherwise, he'd be in hell telling stories to other poor souls about how he was giving it up in the streets. Though he'd survived the fall from the rooftop of Nate's crib, he winded up with a broken arm and a couple of hours spent inside of the hospital. They fixed his arm with a solid cast and sent him on his way with a prescription for pain killaz. As soon as he was released, he hit up Assassin and told him what had gone down. Assassin was pleased with the assassination of Nate, but he was definitely disappointed he and the others hadn't managed to take Hellraiser out the game. Needless to say, Vato felt like a complete failure since he couldn't accomplish what was expected of him. Although the young nigga's ego had taken a blow, Assassin's promise of him having a bright future within his organization had cushioned it.

Vato was eager to get back out in the streets to find Hellraiser and get rid of him once and for all. But Assassin figured he'd done enough for the day and decided to let him rest for a few days. He tried protesting, but Assassin wasn't budging on his decision. He PayPal'd him a few racks to hold him over and told him he'd hit him up when he needed him again.

Vato was bitching and complaining once he'd finally hung up with Assassin, but he then he started softening up to the idea of being off work with pay. He figured he'd blow mad trees, play some Madden, and knock down this bad little beezy that stayed across the hall from him. Shorty had been giving him crazy rhythm, but he'd been on a paper chase something serious, so he had to put smashing her on the back burner. Now that he had a minute to kick his feet up and relax, he was going to devote some time to finally waxing that ass.

Yeah, I'ma hit up shorty right now and see what's up with it, Vato thought with a smile as he walked down the steps of a trap spot. He'd just copped three ounces of purple Kush and intended on copping a bottle of whatever little mama across the hall was in the mood for.

"What up, mamas? What chu got cracking tonight?" Vato asked as he unlocked his navy-blue Audi truck with the black remote control attached to his car keychain. "Why don't chu slide through tonight? We can order a lil' something to eat. Smoke a lil' something, drank a lil' something. Matter fact, what chu like sipping on?"

Vato jumped in behind the wheel of his luxury SUV and slammed the door shut. As soon as he cranked it up, Moneybagg Yo blasted from the speakers. He turned down the volume so he could finish his conversation, pulled out into the street, and drove off down the block.

***

OG was laid back on his bunk reading *The 48 Laws of Power* while Kyjuan did pushups on the floor. The prison went on immediate lockdown once the young gangsta had poked up Big Craig. So, they did what they normally did when they couldn't move around the facility freely.

"Two-hundred and ninety-eight, two-hundred and ninety-nine, three hundred!" Kyjuan called out with his straining voice. He'd pushed himself to his limits to finish the pushups before he hopped to his feet. He snatched up a towel and wiped down his sweaty face and body. His slender physique was pronounced with muscles and heavily tatted.

Hearing something at his back, Kyjuan looked over his shoulder and found a folded up kite peeking underneath the cell's door. Instantly, he knew that the message had come from one of the corrections officers on OG's payroll. The CO was supposed to tell him Big Craig's condition after he'd made his move on him. Kyjuan tossed his towel over his shoulder and picked up the kite. He unfolded it and looked it over. It simply read: expired! Afterwards, he tore the paper into tiny pieces and flushed it.

"Yo, OG, we just got word, that fat nigga, Big Craig, is gone," Kyjuan told him.

"Oh, yeah? That's the news you just got in that kite?" OG asked without taking his eyes off his book.

"Yep." Kyjuan nodded. "I love you, Pops. And any nigga that violates you is violating me. And they're gonna get dealt with, my right hand to God! I don't give a fuck who it is! I love you, OG! You family! You like a father to me, straight up."

OG's eyes were focused on his book, but he was listening to Kyjuan. He couldn't help comparing his rant to the one Rico had in the *Paid in Full* movie after he'd bodied Calvin.

OG took a breath and removed his eyeglasses. He looked over the bunk at Kyjuan. "I love you too, my young nigga. But I think you should try to keep the body count down. You fuck around and catch a charge and you'll never see sunlight again."

"OG, you musta forgotten. I'm not ever gon' see the light of day again. I'm in this bitch for life," Kyjuan reminded him. "I figure while I'm here I'ma live like a king and carve out my legacy. You feel me?"

"Indeed I do," OG replied. "And although you gotta lifetime in here, I know you not tryna see that needle, are you?"

"Mannn, I don't give a fuck! It is what it is!" Kyjuan spoke from the heart. "I'll take whatever these crackaz give me—just make sho' they bury me a G."

"I hear you, youngin'," OG assured him. "You seem so anxious to throw your life away, though. Life is precious. Surely, you've got someone outside of these walls that cares about you."

Unbeknownst to Kyjuan, a couple of days ago, OG had been diagnosed with cancer. After being sentenced to a lifetime of imprisonment and discovering he had a cancer eating away at his body, OG started looking at things a lot differently than he had before. And he was hoping to get Kyjuan to look at things through a clearer lens also. He had a feeling his trying to reason with the young nigga would fall on deaf ears, but he figured it was still worth a shot.

Kyjuan looked down, nodded, and pulled on his nose. He looked back up at OG and licked his lips before responding.

"Yeah, I've got my relatives on the outside," he confessed. "They still hit me on the jack and put money on my books— although I don't really need it. I'll tell you right now if it wasn't for them, I woulda been took myself out. I love my folks to death. Ain't nothing I wouldn't do for 'em, for real, for real."

"That's good. That's real good, son," OG assured him. "It's the love of my family that keeps me—" He was cut short by his going into a coughing fit with his hand over his mouth. His face was balled up and there were veins across his forehead.

Kyjuan frowned, hearing the old man's coughing. "Yo, Pops, are you all right? That's a pretty nasty cough you got there. Sounds like you're tryna hurl up a lung."

OG looked at the palm of his hand and saw blood in it. He wiped it on his pants leg and cleared his throat. "I think—I think I'm coming down with the flu."

"You know, now that I think about it, you have been looking a lil' green around the gills."

"Yeah, you know the health care in this place ain't worth two squirts of piss. So, I figure I'd go ahead and thug it out, as you youngstas say."

"Well, if it's just the flu then I guess you'll eventually get over it."

"No doubt," OG replied as he closed his book and set it aside. He then stretched out and closed his eyes.

"Love you, old man," Kyjuan told him and interlocked his fingers behind his head.

"I love you too—*killa*," OG said with a smirk.

The lights inside of the cell went out!

"Hahahahaha!" Kyjuan, with his eyes closed, laughed. He then listened as OG went into another coughing fit.

Cancer my ass, old nigga, you're not fooling nobody, Kyjuan thought. *You're on your last leg, and should I get the word, I'm gonna sweep it out from under you.*

Kyjuan took a breath and a devilish grin formed on his lips.

***

Inglewood Park Cemetery

Arnez's funeral fell on a gloomy and cold Thursday afternoon. It had stopped raining thirty minutes ago, so the entire cemetery was wet and the dirt road was moist. Surprisingly, Arnez didn't have any family besides Zekey and the Jameses, but his homegoing was packed. Pimps, players, prostitutes, dope boys, thugs, and gangstas from all over came out to pay their last respects to him.

Hellraiser and Da Crew sat together while Zekey and his family sat together on the other side of the room. Zekey sat with his arms hung around Ali and Quan's shoulders. He stared ahead with pink eyes and tears streaming down his face. He was heartbroken and stricken with grief. Today was going to be his last time seeing Arnez, and he wasn't sure how he was going to cope with it.

"You alright, Pops?" Ali asked as he looked up at Zekey. He was in a plum-colored suit and black tie while his step father was wearing a beige turtleneck and black blazer. Zekey looked down at his stepson with a half-hearted grin and nodded. "You know we love you, right? Me and Momma."

"Yeah, I know, son. I love y'all too," Zekey replied with another half-hearted grin and kissed him on the top of his head.

Overhearing Ali and Zekey's interaction brought a smile to a teary-eyed Quan's face. She dabbed her wet eyes, took her husband by the chin, and turned him towards her. Taking the dry end of her Kleenex, she dabbed the wetness from his eyes and cheeks. He grinned at her, and she kissed his lips.

"Are you gonna be okay?" Quan asked with a sniffle.

"Mmmmhmmm," Zekey said with a nod. "How about you?"

When he asked this, the tears seemed to pour out of Quan's eyes nonstop. She dabbed away her tears with the Kleenex and sniffed the green snot back up her right nostril. Zekey hugged her closely and kissed her twice on the side of her face.

"I'll—I'll be fine. I'll be fine," Quan said with a nod, folding her tissue again and dabbing her eyes. "It's just that—I'm really gonna miss 'em, you know? Arnez was a good kid. I'll never forget what he did for me—ever."

***

Zekey and Quan didn't hold back anything from each other. They told each other everything about themselves including the least flattering things. For instance, Quan revealed to him that her ex-husband was an ex-marine with a mean streak that had her walking around him on eggshells. He suffered from PTSD and self-medicated with pain killaz and booze. He'd often taken his issues out on their thirteen-year-old son, Ali, by punching on him like he was a grown-ass man. Often, she'd come home from work to find their son with a black eye, bloody nose, or bruising of some sort. Of course, little homie tried to fight back, but he was hardly a match for a six-foot-one, 225-pound man. When Quan confronted her ex-husband, Devon, about the abuse, he got into her ass too. He called her all kinds of fat, sloppy body bitches and nearly beat her to death.

The beating left Quan barely clinging to life, but after she recovered she still stayed. Devon was the breadwinner. He paid for mostly everything. She knew the money she made as a nursing assistant wasn't hardly enough for her to live on her own, so she stayed through all the drama and the beatings. During the time she was still married to Devon, she was talking to Zekey on the low through a cellphone he'd extorted from another convict. They'd chop it up hours upon hours when Devon was holed up inside some shitty bar getting shit-faced. As much as they talked, they never ran out of things to converse about. It was like there was always something that happened in the past or present that one of them had remembered to tell the other.

Soon, Quan started going down to the prison once a month to visit Zekey. They'd seen each other through pictures, but she'd sent him a photo of her when she was slimmer than she was then. She was terrified of him rejecting her because she was a big girl, so it took some persuading from her homegirl to get her to finally go see him. Her friend, Gabby, beat her face and made sure her hair was laid to the gods. She picked out the perfect outfit that showed off all her curves and complemented her ample breasts and beach-ball-sized butt. Gabby even hit her with two sprays of her intoxicating perfume that was a straight-up Man Killa. The fragrance was known to bring any man under its spell and have him eating out of the palm of its wearer's hand.

When Quan met Zekey, it was love at first sight. They were feeling each other. Her weight wasn't even a problem. He loved BBWs. He revealed to her that his ex-girlfriend, Yoyo, was a plus-size woman. In fact, mostly all the women he'd been with were full figured. Quan and Zekey had fallen in love. And in time, Ali had fallen in love with him too. They talked almost as often as she and Zekey did. It got to a point that the little dude started referring to him as Pops. They developed a bond like no other.

Quan started sending Zekey money out of her paycheck every week for his necessities. He had refused to take her money at first, but she eventually convinced him to accept it. He promised when he came home that he was going to take care of her and Ali. That she'd never have to punch a clock again once he was on the outside and had gotten his shit together. Quan believed him wholeheartedly. Her mind was telling her she was a damn fool and Zekey was running that prison game on her like so many brothas on lock ran on sisters. Her heart was telling her something different altogether, though. Her heart was telling her to love, trust, support, and believe in him. That he was going to be the man that changed how she felt about being in love, so that's what she did.

A year down the line, Devon became wise to Quan and Zekey's relationship. Enraged, he beat her so viciously she winded up in the hospital and Ali winded up staying with his grandmother while she was recovering. Quan told the doctor tending to her that her husband was the one that had beaten her to a pulp. She even told him how he was whipping on their son. The doctor alerted the authorities and a cop showed up to take down her report. Devon *was eventually picked up, but an old war buddy of his posted bail. He started stalking Quan. He'd park outside of her mother's house for hours or send death threats over the phone.*

Devon's terrorizing of Quan started driving her crazy. She started losing her hair and mad weight. She found it hard to eat, sleep, and even function in public. Everywhere she went she thought Devon's nut ass was going to pop up out of nowhere and kill her. It got so bad that she was scared of leaving the house, and when she would, she'd pack a big-ass butcher's knife in her purse.

Quan kept all of this from Zekey for months. She didn't want to add to his stress level while he was incarcerated. But one day, during one of their routine phone calls, he could tell by the tremble in her voice that something was terribly wrong. It took some time, but he was eventually able to coerce her to tell him what was up. Once she finally did, he went deathly silent on the phone.

"Babe, are you still there?" Quan asked.

"Yeah, I'm still here, lil' mama," Zekey replied then cleared his throat. "Look, you not finna have to worry about dude no more. That I promise you."

"Zeek, what're you gonna do?" she asked with worry evident in her voice.

"Don't worry about all of that," he told her sternly. "Just know your days of being homeboy's punching bag are over. That's on everything I love, real shit."

"Okay."

"I'ma have someone come holla at chu. So, make sure you're home tomorrow evening."

"Alright, baby. I'll be here," she assured him. "I love you, Zekey."

"I love you too, lil' mama. You're the best thang to ever happen to a nigga," he admitted. "I really mean that."

"Awww, muah!" she smooched him over the jack.

"Muah!" he smooched her back. "I gotta go, babe. It's time for count."

***

The Next Day/Evening

Quan was washing the dishes when the doorbell chimed. She dried her hands off with a towel and tossed it over her shoulder as she made her way towards the front door. The doorbell chimed once again!

"Hold on. I'm coming," Quan called out to whoever it was at the door. She unlocked it and pulled it open. She found Arnez and KiMani standing on the other side. KiMani was rocking his street clothes while Arnez was in his all-black murder gear. Although they looked really young, their demeanors were definitely intimidating to Quan.

"How're you doing? I'm Arnez, Zekey's nephew," Arnez introduced himself and shook her hand. "And this is my brother, KiMani."

"Hi," Quan said, shaking KiMani's hand.

"What's up?" KiMani greeted her as he shook her hand.

"Well, come on in." Quan stepped aside and waved them inside. Once they crossed the threshold, she closed and locked the door behind them. When she turned around, she saw them admiring her home.

"Nice place you got here," Arnez complimented her home.

"Thank you," a smiling Quan replied.

Arnez picked up a portrait of her, Zekey, and Ali from a nearby shelf. Zekey was in a blue prison uniform with CDC on it. He had one arm around Quan while the other was around Ali. They were all smiling, looking like the perfect family. Arnez cracked a one-sided smile. He thought he'd never see the day when his big homie would become a family man.

"Mannn, look at this nigga Zekey, Blood, who woulda thought?" Arnez turned to show KiMani the portrait. KiMani glanced at it but didn't say shit. He never fucked with Zekey ever since he tried to peel his cap that night. Hell, the only reason why he was there now was to back Arnez. If it wasn't for him, then he wouldn't have come along on the mission. Zekey and his bitch would have to handle their own affairs.

Seeing that KiMani wasn't interested in the portrait, Arnez dropped the one-sided smile and placed the portrait back where he'd picked it up from.

"It smells good in here. What chu was cooking?" Arnez asked Quan.

"Fried chicken, biscuits, mixed veggies, and rice," she replied. "I have leftovers if you guys would like some."

"Yeah. I'd like some. A nigga ain't ate all day," Arnez said with his hand on his stomach.

"How about chu, sweetie?" Quan said to KiMani. He was about to say no because he didn't fuck with everybody's food, but his stomach just so happened to growl. "That means yes." She smiled and headed toward the kitchen. "Y'all have a seat while I heat your food up in the oven," she told them.

Arnez and KiMani followed her inside of the kitchen where they sat at the table. She served them their plates of food once it was done warming in the oven and poured them a glass of lemonade Crystal Light. She sat down at the table with them and watched as they began to eat.

"Yo, fill us in on the shit you've been going through with this nigga," Arnez said as he sat up with a cheek full of food, holding his glass.

"Okay," Quan agreed. She cleared her throat and started telling them about Devon and all of the abuse he put her and their son through. They listened attentively as they stuffed their faces and drank from their glasses of lemonade. The more she told them, the more heated they got. The expressions on their faces told it all. Her story fueled them to do what they were requested to do that night, and that was exactly what they wanted.

Quan broke down sobbing with a snotty nose, while relaying her horrific experiences with her husband. KiMani handed her the paper towels she'd given him to wipe his hands with. She used them to wipe her wet cheeks and blow her nose. Arnez swallowed his food, wiped his hands and then his mouth before pushing away from the table. He walked over to Quan and threw his arm around her shoulder, comforting her.

"Everything is gon' be alright, goddess," Arnez assured her. *"You know you fucking with my unc, so that makes you and yo' lil' one family. And family takes care of family,"* he told her. *"I assure you that after tonight, your troubles of today will be a thing of the past. Ain't that right, my nigga, Ki."* He looked at KiMani, who was taking a sip of his glass of lemonade.

KiMani sat his glass down on the table top and raised his right hand. *"My right hand to God."*

"Now look," Arnez said, kneeling down to Quan and taking her chubby hands into his. *"I needa picture of this nigga and a couple of spots he frequents. You think you can cover that?"*

Quan nodded and continued to wipe her eyes with the balled-up paper towels. *"There's a picture of him on top of the refrigerator. I put it there once I knew you guys were coming,"* she informed him. Arnez looked to KiMani and nodded to the fridge. KiMani took the picture down, looked at it, and then passed it to Arnez for him to take a look at.

"This it?" Arnez asked her as he held up the picture for her to see. She nodded. He took another look at the picture. It was of a younger and more in-shape Devon in his green, military-issued cap, suit, and tie. One side of his suit's jacket was loaded with medals he'd earned during his time in the army.

"Where this nigga be at?" KiMani asked, walking up beside Quan, placing his hand on her shoulder.

"Right now, he's over at this dive called The Bar Fly. It's on the lower eastside," Quan informed them. *"It's his favorite spot. He's always there around this time."*

Arnez stood upright and slid the picture inside of his back pocket. *"Alright, Mamas, me and my brother gon' take care of this. You're gonna need an alibi though. 'Cause once I pop this dude, the first person the cops are gonna investigate is you. His wife. What I need for you to do is go someplace where there are a lotta people that can see you."*

"Yeah, I'd say a movie theater," KiMani told her. *"It's plenty of cameras there and plenty of people to see you. Plus, you'll have a ticket that will verify that you were there."*

"Good thinking, bro," Arnez said, pointing his finger at Ki-Mani.

"No doubt." KiMani nodded.

"Yeah, Mama, do just that," Arnez told Quan. "By the way, where's yo' lil' man, Ali?"

"He's at his friend's house, next door," Quan said, blowing her nose.

"Smooth," Arnez replied. "Be sure to call his people and let them know you're stepping out. Them knowing your whereabouts will help witcho alibi."

"Okay." Quan nodded and wiped her snotty nose. "I'm gonna grab my purse and head out now."

"Alright," Arnez said.

Quan stood upright and abruptly hugged him. She buried her face into his hoodie and broke down crying again. He hushed her and rubbed her back soothingly. KiMani stood by, watching them with a mad dog look across his face. He'd been abused mentally and physically as well. So he was going to take pride in the murder he'd be participating in that night.

***

The night was cool with the occasional breeze. The only sounds were that of the traffic, a car driving by every now and again. There was prolonged silence and then a man twenty-seven years of age shuffled out of a locally known establishment called The Bar Fly. He was a light-skinned brother with a military-style haircut he needed touched up and a nappy beard. His eyes were glassy and red webbed. He was literally pissy drunk. The wet spot at the front of his denim jeans portrayed this as well as his slurred speech and wobbly legs. He was moving around on them like a newborn fawn, fresh out of its mother's womb. Though he was having trouble maintaining his balance, his cane supported his teetering equilibrium.

"Ol' dick-sucking ass nigga, gon' tell me I've had enough," Devon slurred and wiped his dripping lip. He was bitching about the bartender because he'd refused to serve him any more alcohol on the account he was entirely too wasted. "I'ma grown-ass man, I know when I've hadda 'nough." He looked down at the wet spot at the crotch of his jeans. His brows furrowed and he narrowed his eyes. "Well, I'll be goddamn. I done pissed myself like a newborn baby, son of a bitch!"

Devon wobbled over to the curb, looking up and down the street for the cab the bartender had ordered for him. Although he was standing in one place, he was tilting north, south, east, and west. This wasn't solely due to his inebriated state, either. The shrapnel he'd caught in his right kneecap from an explosion while on tour in Iraq aided his handicap. It was the reason he'd gotten honorably discharged from the marines and received those monthly checks from Uncle Sam.

"I wonder if this that damn cab Nigel ordered for me," Devon said, looking down the street at an approaching vehicle. A black-on-black, '96 Chevy Caprice was coasting up on him. Its lights were out, so he held his hand above his brow trying to make out the silhouette on the driver's side. Once he saw it wasn't a yellow cab, he knew it wasn't his ride. As he dropped his hand at his side, he locked eyes with the driver. He was a young man that looked like he wasn't old enough to drink or drive. Devon figured the little nigga had stolen the whip for a joy ride. "Young, punk-ass niggaz always taking other people's shit. Then wonder why the goddamn police are shooting their black asses down like dogs in the street. When will they learn?" He belched as he craned his neck, continuously following the Caprice.

"Say, OG, you gotta light?" a voice came from over Devon's shoulder. As soon as he looked behind him, it was like firecrackers exploded in his face. He dropped his cane and fell awkwardly to the sidewalk, with his left leg tucked under him. Arnez, the masked gunman, walked up on him and gave him four more shots to the dome for good measure. He then tucked his gun inside of his hoodie and casually strolled away. He scanned the area as he walked to make sure no one had seen him do the Devil's work.

Arnez made a right at the end of the block and hopped into the passenger seat of a Chevy Caprice. He slammed the door shut, and the driver, KiMani, drove away. A moment later, several patrons, including the bartender, Nigel, emerged out of The Bar Fly. They walked up on a dead Devon. His blood was pouring out of all the holes in his head and seeping into the cracks and crevices of the sidewalk.

Nigel bumped his way through the crowd until he was standing over Devon's body. A frown came over his face as he kneeled down to him. He shook his head and crossed himself in the sign of the Holy crucifix.

"Aye, did anyone order an Uber?" a man called out from a white 2012 Nissan Sentra. Nigel and the patrons looked up at him. He was entirely too late!

After Arnez had laid his murder game down, sure enough, the cops came around asking Quan questions. Her alibi checked out, so they eventually left her alone. A week later, she received a fat ass check from the life insurance company. She paid for Devon's funeral, all her bills, and got herself and Ali a few things. She tried to drop a bag on Arnez and KiMani, but they refused her generosity, stating it was all love.

One month later, Zekey proposed to Quan during one of her many visits. She picked out her ring and he paid for it with money he'd been extorting from niggaz in prison. A year later, the two of them got married and became Mr. and Mrs. Ezekiel Whitmore.

Chapter Seven

Quan dried her eyes again and blew her nose into the Kleenex. She balled the tissue up and Zekey kissed and hugged her. She closed her eyes and snuggled against him. They heard the minister up at the podium going on and on, but they were paying little attention to him. They were more so consumed in the moment and their own thoughts. Zekey's forehead furrowed when he looked over Quan's head and saw Hellraiser and Da Crew. He couldn't believe he hadn't noticed them until now. But then again, the place was so overcrowded you couldn't make anyone out among the attendees.

"Look who's here," Zekey told Quan. Her brows furrowed, wondering, and he nodded. When she looked over her shoulder, she saw Hellraiser and them.

"I'm surprised they decided to come," she said, looking at them.

"Not me. I'm finna go holla at 'em real quick." He kissed her twice on the lips. When he went to rise, she pulled him back down and dried his face with a fresh bunch of Kleenexes. Afterwards, he said a bunch of 'excuse me's' as he came across people sitting in the pew. A couple of them had obituaries, which they were fanning themselves with.

Zekey locked eyes with Hellraiser when he finally cleared the row of pews. He motioned him over and watched as he whispered something to Lachaun, who was sitting beside him. She waved at Zekey and he waved back. Hellraiser kissed Lachaun on the cheek, said something to Lil' Saint and Mack, and then made his way out of the row of pews. He was wearing an ebony suit with a red bandana-print tie and matching Hush Puppies. When he emerged from the pews, he slapped hands with Zekey and pulled him in for an embrace, patting him on his back.

"I'm glad you decided to come," Zekey told him as they walked toward the back of the room.

"Nothing short of death could have kept me from coming to pay my respect to Arnez," Hellraiser assured him, as they made their way outside where several other people were gathered, talking. There wasn't enough room for them to get inside the service, so they decided to kick it outside until it was time to view the body. "He wassa good kid, and on top of that, he was my boy's best friend."

"Speaking of your boy... How is he?"

Hellraiser took a breath and said, "He's still inna coma, but he'll pull through. Our lineage is fulla warriors. The Jameses don't go down without putting up one hell of a fight."

"What y'all doing out here?" Lil' Saint asked as he stepped outside. He was as sharp as a coyote's fangs in his beige three-piece suit and powder blue tie.

"Just holla at cha boy here," Hellraiser said as he placed his hand on Zekey's shoulder. "Saint, this is Zekey. Zekey, this is Saint."

"I'm familiar with Saint. What up, Blood?" Zekey said, dapping him up.

"How do you know Saint?" Hellraiser asked out of curiosity.

"Man, I know all of y'all. I grew up on 27th Street and went to Jefferson High School," Zekey informed them. "You, your wife, Chaun Dog, Saint, Mack, and Julian, y'all make up Da Crew. Y'all niggaz are legends in the streets," he told them. "Y'all gotta few years on me, but I've seen y'all around the hood...well, when I wasn't locked inside The Beast."

Lil' Saint cast his eyes at the ground as he massaged his chin, thinking for a moment. When a light bulb came on inside his head, he snapped his fingers. "Killa Zeek?"

"Yeah, that's me," Zekey said with a slight grin on his lips. Their hood was so big that everyone didn't know each other. The homies mostly stuck to the niggaz who were under their clique. A clique was like a gang within a gang.

"I've heard about cho work. You don't mess around," Lil' Saint told him.

"From what I hear, neither does Da Crew."

There was a moment of silence and then Hellraiser spoke again.

"Aye, where's Mack?"

"Probably in the men's room checking his draws," Lil' Saint replied. ·

Hellraiser's forehead creased. "What do you mean?"

"Mannnn, that fool was in there letting off, got it stanking in there something awful," Lil' Saint said. "That's why I came out here to see what y'all were doing."

"I told that nigga to lay off that Mexican food," Hellraiser said with a grin.

***

Mack sat in the half-empty row of pews, grimacing, holding his stomach and tapping his foot. A twin was on either side of him. One was frowning from his foul stench and fanning herself while the other was spraying some perfume to mask the smell. Once she'd finished, she placed the perfume back inside her handbag and zipped it closed.

"You okay, daddy?" the twin with the obituary asked with concern.

"Nah, man, I knew I shouldn't have eaten those damn enchiladas. I gotta go to the restroom," Mack said as he jumped to his dress-shoed feet and ran towards the aisle, farting like a mothafucka. He let one rip for so long that bitch sounded like an AK-47 firing until it was empty.

Aw, fuck, aw, fuck, aw, fuck! Please, lemme make it to the restroom. I'm too goddamn old to be shitting on myself, Mack thought as he hauled ass down the hallway, unbuckling his belt and then unzipping his slacks. He held up his slacks with one hand while he ran, steadily farting. He rounded the corner and saw the men's restroom ahead. Once he'd gotten close enough, he jumped into the air and kicked the restroom's door open. The door banged off the wall and he darted inside to the last stall. He pushed his way in, locked the door, and allowed his slacks to drop in a pile at his dress shoes.

Mack danced around and he withdrew a toilet seat protector from the box hanging over the commode. He placed the protector on the seat as perfectly as he could before plopping down on it. As soon as his bear ass graced the toilet seat, he unloaded and sighed with relief. He farted and then unloaded some more.

"Goddamn, I nearly shitted on myself. Whew." He wiped the beaded sweat from his forehead and pulled out his cellular. He figured since he didn't have any reading material that he'd entertain himself with social media. "Man, all these young hoes do is shake ass on IG. Ain't got shit going for themselves besides pussy and likes," he said to himself, shaking his head in disappointment.

Just then, the men's restroom opened as two men in suits walked inside talking. They stepped up to the urinals, but they were sure to stay two urinals down from each other.

"So, what chu gon' do witcho cut, Ty?" the man wearing the flat top and off-the-rack suit asked his coworker.

"Catch up with my child support so I can get Kim's funky ass off my back, nigga," the man with the bald head said. He was wearing a velvet button-up shirt and tie. "And I guess a few thangs for lil' Drew."

"Man, who woulda thought twenty bands would fall in our lap and all we hadda do was place that bomb inside ol' boy's coffin."

When Mack overheard this, he stopped scrolling through Instagram and gave their conversation his undivided attention. He was listening closely with his eyes bulging and his mouth hanging open.

"Speaking of bomb, ain't that bitch set to go in like ten minutes?" Miles asked, zipping up his slacks and walking over to the line of sinks against the wall alongside Tyler.

"Nah, more like..." Tyler glanced at his timepiece and his eyebrows rose. "Shit, I say, uh, eight minutes. We better be getting the fuck from outta here."

Tyler and Miles quickly soaped up their hands and began rinsing them. They were startled when the last stall door flew open and Mack came running out like he had the KKK on his black ass. He tackled open the men's room door and spilled out onto the hallway, landing on his side. He grimaced, having knocked the wind out of himself, but quickly scrambled to his feet. He pulled up his slacks and adjusted them on his waist as he ran full speed ahead back to the area where Arnez's funeral was being held.

"There's a bomb—there's a mothafucking bomb in the building!" Mack yelled as loud as he could with beads of sweat sliding down the sides of his face.

"Brotha, what is the meaning of this?" the minister approached Mack, speaking into the microphone. The people in the room were looking around, confused. Some of them were even smiling and/or laughing. They thought Mack was just fucking around, but they'd soon find out he wasn't.

"Gemme this goddamn mic!" Mack growled at the minister, snatching the microphone out of his hand, and shoved his big ass. The minister stumbled backwards and nearly fell. He whipped around to the audience and addressed them through the microphone. "I'm not bullshitting with y'all! There's a bomb in this coffin." He pointed at Arnez's coffin. "It's set to blow inna few minutes, so get cho families and get the fuck outta here!" He threw the microphone down to the floor and ran over to the coffin. He felt around it and then looked underneath for the bomb. He frowned when he didn't find one. At this time, people were taking their time getting out of the funeral home while the twins were coming up to Mack. Mack opened the upper half of the coffin and looked inside at Arnez. He looked peacefully asleep.

Mack opened the other half of the coffin with the twins standing on either side of him, wondering what was up with the bomb situation. Hellraiser, Zekey, and Lil' Saint bumped their way through the flood of people heading towards the entrance. They were wearing serious looks as they marched down the aisle. Zekey and Hellraiser swapped a few words with their wives, kissed them goodbye, and directed them towards the door. They then jogged towards the coffin where Mack and the twins were.

Mack had just finished giving the inside of the coffin a thorough inspection, and he still couldn't find the bomb. He was sweating like one of them niggaz in the bomb squad now, and his heart was thudding like a cornered rodent. He wiped the sweat from his forehead, removed his suit's jacket, and slung it aside. Next, he glanced at his Rolex for the time and looked at Arnez. "I'm sorry about this, kid, but I'm tryna save lives here." With that said, Mack pushed the coffin over, and Arnez came rolling out.

The people that were still inside the room gasped and hollered, seeing what he'd done. They still didn't think they were in any real danger.

"Say, bruh, what the fuck is up witcho man?" Zekey asked Hellraiser with a scowl.

"I don't know, but we're about to find out," Hellraiser said as they reached Mack. "Yo, Mack, what's up?"

Mack explained to them all what was going on as he kneeled down to the coffin and pulled out a Swiss army knife, which was attached to his car keys. He pulled out the blade of his shiny knife and cut into the fabric lining the coffin. Still holding the Swiss army knife, he tore the fabric out of it, knocked on the bottom of it until he heard a space that wasn't so hollow, and then started kicking it. *Bwrack!* A hole as big as a basketball appeared. Mack sat his car keys aside and reached inside the hole. He had a very concentrated look across his face as he felt around inside the hole for the bomb.

"Where are they, Mack? Where the two niggaz you overheard talking?" Hellraiser asked him while he and Zekey held their guns at their sides. While Hellraiser was asking all the questions, Zekey and Lil' Saint were looking around for anyone wearing guilty expressions. They would then know they were involved with the placement of the bomb.

"I don't know where them two niggaz are, but I did overhear them say their names," Mack replied with a strained voice as he continued to feel around in the bottom of the coffin. "They—they work here. One is—is Miles and—and the other name is Ty. So, I'm guessing his government is—is either Tyler or—or Taylor."

"If these fools are involved, then chances are the director is too," Zekey said. "As a matter of fact, I'ma see if I can catch up with either one of 'em." He patted Hellraiser on the shoulder, dapped up Lil' Saint, and ran off to see if he could find the men

Mack had mentioned. He remembered the faces of the men who were standing present when he'd first arrived there. They were a couple of younger cats that were thirty or so in age and dressed in cheap suits.

"I've got it! I've got the bomb!" Mack announced, holding up a big black explosive device weighing about five pounds. When the people who were trying to get out of the room heard him and saw the bomb in his hand, they broke their necks trying to get out of there. They were damn near crawling over each other trying to get through the entrance.

"How much time does it have left on it?" one of the twins asked.

Mack took a look at the timer on the bomb. His eyes widened, and his heart thudded harder. "Aw, fuck, awwww, fuck!"

"What's wrong, daddy?" the other twin asked.

Mack showed them all the timer of the bomb. It read: 3:00, then 2:59.

"Shit just got real," Hellraiser said, seeing the time on the bomb.

"Father, help us," Lil' Saint said, seeing the timer winding down.

At this time, they could hear the emergency sirens approaching from afar.

"I've seen one of these babies in a documentary on Discovery channel," Mack said. "It has enough nitro to level a building six times this size."

A grim look was on everyone's faces hearing what danger they were all in. A bomb squad wouldn't make it there in time to deactivate the explosive, so they had to get it away from the area as soon as possible.

"What're you gonna do?" Hellraiser asked him. Mack gave him a knowing look and right then, he knew what he had in mind. They all did for that matter.

Mack hugged Hellraiser, Lil' Saint, and the twins, who were on the verge of tears. The girls knew that Mack was going to try to get the bomb as far away from the area as possible. They only feared he wouldn't get away from the bomb before it exploded.

When Mack went to break the twins' embrace they held fast, not wanting to let go of him. "Alright, y'all, I gotta go before this mothafucka explodes!" Mack said, pulling away from the twins and taking off running. Seeing the entrance was crowded and the bomb's timer had two and a half minutes left, he hauled ass back in the opposite direction, passing Hellraiser and them. The back exit was crowded with people trying to get the fuck out of the tenement too.

"Fuck, fuck, what am I gonna do? Think, think, think, think!" Mack said to no one particular, smacking himself upside the head. Coming up with something, he snatched his gun from his shoulder holster and busted up at the ceiling.

Poc, poc, poc, poc!

Debris trickled down from the ceiling and onto the floor. The people crowding the back entrance screamed and hollered in a panic. The terror that being shot brought them had their asses shoving and pushing each other out the way. Mack saw a path clearing for him, so he ran forward, busting shot after shot into the ceiling. People started shoving each other out the way, trying to get out of the funeral home. Mack, with the bomb tucked under his arm, came running out of the funeral home like he was Walter Payton. He glanced at the timer on the bomb and saw he had two minutes left.

"Shiiiiit!" Mack cussed and looked around for his car. He wiped the beads of sweat from his forehead and ran forth. With four big steps, he was on top of someone's Ford Explorer and scanning the area for his whip. Once he zeroed in on it, he jumped on the truck's hood and then onto the ground. He took off running towards his car, coming across people screaming and zig zagging across his line of vision.

Huffing and puffing, Mack ran toward his whip, wiping his sweaty forehead. He ran past a man who had just hopped behind the wheel of his royal blue 2015 Porsche 918 Spyder. The sports car was far faster than his Cadillac, so he knew he'd have a better chance clearing the area in it.

Mack ran back to the driver's side window of the Porsche. The man looked at him like, *What the fuck do you want?*

"Say, homie, I needa borrow yo' car," Mack told him.

The man gave Mack the middle finger and fired up his whip, revving that bitch up. Mack scowled and knocked on the window with the butt of his gun. Once he had his attention, he pointed his banga in his face and his ass looked spooked.

"Get cho bitch ass out the car, nigga!" Mack roared and spit flew from his mouth, dotting up the driver's window.

"Okay, okay, bruh! Chill, chill, chill!" The man bowed down, holding up one hand in surrender and popping open the door with the other. As soon as the door cracked open, Mack tucked his blower and yanked him out of the sports car by his tie. The man fell to the ground and quickly scrambled back up on his feet, running away.

Mack jumped behind the wheel of the sports car, sat the bomb on the center console, and sped backwards. He was about to take off when one of the twins snatched open the passenger door and hopped in. Her sister hopped in on her lap and they slammed the door shut.

"What the fuck are y'all doing?" Mack asked with a frown and buckled his safety belt.

"Daddy, we're going with you. No matter what, we stick together," the twin said that was sitting in the passenger seat.

"That's right, daddy. We ride or die," the twin chimed in that was sitting on her sister's lap. They both outstretched their wrists and turned them over so their tattoos would show. Ride or Die. Mack had the same ink on the inside of his wrist. He had all the girls that were hoing for him get the branding, but they all eventually jumped ship. Not the twins though! They stayed down with him whether times were good or bad. That's why he retired them from the game and married them on some bigamy shit. These last few years, he'd been showering them with time, affection, and the finer things in life.

Mack looked at their tattoos and grinned. He was in love with the twins and their die-hard devotion to him. "Ride or Die," he replied and extended his wrist, turning it over to the identical tattoo he shared with them.

Vrooooom!

The Porsche 918 Spyder sped up the cemetery's wet road, splashing mud everywhere. The hand of the speedometer swept around fast, and the sports car growled like an angry grizzly. The whip was going so fast that the wind was ruffling everyone's hair and clothing. Occasionally, Mack would glance at the bomb's timer to see how much time he had. When he saw he had sixty seconds left, he glanced back to how far he was from the funeral home. Satisfied with the distance he'd put between himself and the tenement, Mack slammed on the brakes and threw the sports car in park.

"Y'all get out—hurry, girls!" Mack told them with a panicky voice. Instantly, the girls hopped out of the drop-top Spyder. They were about to run away until they saw Mack struggling to unbuckle his safety belt. "Fuck, fuck, fuck!" he cussed up a storm as he struggled to unbuckle himself. He quickly went through his pockets, looking for his car keys, and remembered he'd dropped them back at the funeral home.

"Hold on, daddy. I've gotta switch blade in my purse," one of the twins said, running towards him and fishing through her purse. Coming up with the knife, she triggered its blade and flung her purse aside. Mack threw open the driver's door and the twin with the switch blade got on her knees. The other twin stood by her side, tapping her foot impatiently. Everyone's hearts were beating so fast they thought they'd explode at any moment.

"Fuck! Twenty-five seconds!" Mack called out, seeing the time left on the bomb.

"I'm going as fast as I can, daddy," the twin cutting on his safety belt told him.

"We're not gonna make it in time! That's it! Y'all go, y'all run!" Mack yelled at them.

"No, we're not leaving you, daddy. Ride or Die," the waiting twin said as tears streamed down her cheeks.

"That's right. Ride or Die," the twin cutting the safety belt chimed in. She wiped her dripping eyes and continued to cut against the safety belt.

"Fifteen seconds, girls! That's it. This is the end," Mack said with a defeated voice.

"I love you, daddy," the twin said, finally having finished cutting through the safety belt. Still holding the switch blade, she hugged Mack and cried her eyes out.

"I love you too, daddy," the twin that was standing by waiting said. She kicked off her heels, ran around the Porsche Spyder, and snatched open the passenger door. She hopped into the front passenger seat and left the door wide open. She hugged Mack around his neck, kissed him on the cheek, and grabbed hold of her sister. Her sister kissed Mack right after her.

"I love y'all—both of y'all," Mack told them, kissing them both. They all closed their eyes and bowed their heads. They held each other tightly, waiting for the explosion that would end all of their lives.

***

"Why did they stop? Why the fuck did they stop?" Hellraiser asked Lil' Saint before taking off running. Lil' Saint took off after him. They were running as fast as they could towards Mack and the twins. "Get outta the car! Get the fuck outta the car!" he yelled as loud as he could, waving his hands. "Ooof!" He tripped and fell on the dirt road, muddying his suit. Lil' Saint ran right past him. He hurried back to his feet and kept running towards Mack and them.

Ba-Boooom!

Frooosh!

The Porsche Spyder exploded into burning wreckage and a big ass fireball rocketed up into the sky. The blow back from the explosion sent dirt and debris flying in Hellraiser and Lil' Saint's direction. The forceful wind ruffled their suits and made their ties flap at their backs like laundry hanging on a clothesline on a windy day.

Hellraiser dropped to his knees, bowed his head, and sank his hands into the muddy road. His eyes misted and his chest expanded with every heaving breath he took. He didn't have any more tears to shed after losing another one of his friends. He'd cried until he couldn't cry anymore, so now he wanted a dish that was best served cold. He wanted revenge.

Hellraiser threw his head back, screaming loudly. "Noooooooooooooo!"

Chapter Eight
Night

"Man, shut cho punk ass up, can't nobody hear you screaming out here! We're way out in the middle of fucking nowhere!" Zekey barked at Ty, who he'd taking out the trunk of the Cadillac he and Quan had stolen. Though he couldn't find Ty and Miles at the funeral home, he was able to convince homegirl working in Human Resources to give him their full names and addresses. With that pertinent information in his hands, he was able to kidnap them and get the money they were paid to plant the bomb in Arnez's coffin. At gunpoint, Ty's mark ass even gave up a third party's involvement. The funeral director: Wilt Compton. It turns out old Wilt was Miles' uncle, and he knew exactly where he laid down at night. Zekey didn't waste any time hitting Hellraiser up and having him pick homeboy up. Although Hellraiser wanted to smoke his ass on the spot, Zekey got him to agree to bring him to the location they were at now.

"I don't know how you managed to get this duct tape off yo' mouth, but if you make another sound, I'ma putta hot one right through yo' fucking eye," Zekey said through clenched teeth, as he held him about the throat and pressed his gun into his eye socket. "You got that? Huh?"

"Yeah, man, I got it! I got it!" a terrified Ty assured him with his head held back. Zekey placed the duct tape back over his mouth and smoothed it out.

"Good," Zekey replied and smacked him across the side of the head with his gun. The blow opened up a bloody gash on his forehead, and he dropped down to one knee. Zekey came behind him and kicked him in his ass, sending him face first into the tall dead grass. Ty pulled his face up from the ground, grimacing. There was dirt over his left eye and the side of his face. He narrowed his eyes from the bright headlights of a car idling before him. There was one dark figure standing before the vehicle, but he couldn't make him out.

"Stand up, nigga, and if you try to run, I'ma shoot chu down like a dog in the street," he assured him and dropped the hand he held his gun in at his side. He reached back inside the trunk and pulled out Miles. He still had the duct tape over his mouth and his wrists were bound behind his back like Ty's were. "Stand over there witcho, girlfriend!" He shoved Miles forward and he nearly fell.

"Baby, you need some help with them?" Quan asked while holding her head out the driver's window of the Cadillac.

"Get, nigga!" Zekey kicked Miles so hard in his buttocks that he almost fell. He then spat on the ground, tucked his gun at the small of his back, and made his way over to the driver's window of the Caddy. He rested his arms on the window sill and leaned inside of the car. "Nah, I've got things covered out here, beautiful, but I'll be sure to holla at chu if we need some assistance," he assured her and turned her toward him by her chin. He pressed his lips against hers and slipped her a little tongue. He kissed her deep and lovingly.

Hearing a honking horn behind him, Zekey turned around to see who he believed was Hellraiser taking his hand from out of the driver's window of his car. He assumed he'd just blown the horn for his attention, so he told Quan he'd be right back and headed in his direction. As Zekey approached Hellraiser, he saw the trunk of his car rise. A minute later, it was slamming shut. Then Lil' Saint came walking from the rear of the vehicle with someone big and tall on a chain-linked dog collar.

"What the fuck is going on here?" Zekey asked no one particular. He held his hand above his brows and tried to get a good look at who was holding onto the chain-linked dog collar. It was Lil' Saint!

"You good?" the man that had blown the horn asked Zekey. When he'd gotten closer, Zekey could finally see his face. It was Hellraiser.

"Yeah, I'm straight. You?" Zekey shot back.

Hellraiser nodded and looked over Zekey's shoulder. Quan was hopping from the driver's side of the Cadillac and slamming the door behind her. She made her way to the rear of the whip, cocking the slide on her gun. She then posted up and kept a close eye on Miles and Ty.

"You good over there, ma?" Zekey asked Quan from over his shoulder.

"Yeah, I'm just watching these niggaz. They're moving around a lil' too much for me," Quan replied. She then said something to Miles and Ty that Zekey and Hellraiser couldn't hear. But they assumed she told their hostages to get down on their knees since that's what they were doing now.

"I take it that's Wilt, the funeral director," Zekey said, nodding to the man Lil' Saint was walking over like he was a horse.

"Yeah, that's pale, pasty, white ass," Hellraiser replied, looking over his shoulder at Lil' Saint and the third hostage. As he and Lil' Saint walked past him, he smacked him on his flat ass. He yelped and jumped from the stinging of the swat, which left a red hand impression on his left buttock.

The man on the chained dog leash was six-foot-four with bushy, graying chest hair and a protruding belly. His wrists were handcuffed behind his back. He was wearing a black leather face mask covered with dull spikes and a black thong.

"What's the story behind this cracka smelling like chocolate syrup?" Zekey asked with a frown. He caught a whiff of Wilt as he passed him.

"When we ran up in his crib, him and his lil' skinny-ass Chinese fun boy was getting freaky," Hellraiser replied. "Lil' fuck drew down on me and Saint, so I hadda take 'em off his feet."

"You mean he's dead now?" Zekey asked with a raised eyebrow. Hellraiser answered with a nod. "Fuck 'em! Come on, Blood." He tapped Hellraiser and motioned for him to follow him. They walked over to Miles and Ty, who were on their knees before Quan. Lil' Saint tried to force Wilt down to his knees, but the stubborn son of a bitch wouldn't budge. Zekey and Hellraiser peeped what was going on as they walked up on him. While in motion, Zekey upped his gun and blasted out the back of Wilt's knees.

"Aaaaaaahhh!" Wilt threw his head back, hollering, but the red ball gag blocked the sound. Blood poured out the holes in his kneecaps as he dropped down to them. He became teary eyed and whimpered like a little girl.

"Y'all seem to have gotten it fucked up," Zekey said, walking around Wilt with his smoking gun. His face was balled up angrily, and his trigger finger was itching like it had poison ivy. "Y'all don't run a damn thang, we do!" He swept his hand around to Hellraiser, Lil' Saint, and Quan. "It's y'all that's at the mercy of our guns. Niggaz better start acting like they know!"

Suddenly, Ty jumped up to his feet and took off running for his life. Zekey's head whipped around in his direction as he made hurried footsteps, leaving dirt clouds in his wake. Zekey lifted his gun again and finger fucked the trigger. Bullets puked out of his gun's barrel with sparks flying out behind them. Ty's head snapped backward as his chest exploded in broken bone and blood. He flopped to the ground on his stomach with his legs going up in the air.

"I haven't met a nigga yet that can outrun a bullet," Hellraiser said, seeing Zekey cut down Ty without remorse. He shook his head and looked back over to the remaining hostages that were on their knees.

Miles bowed his head and squeezed his eyes shut. Tears went sliding down his cheeks as his shoulders rocked from his sobbing. His heart was racing awfully fast, and he could feel his blood pressure rising. On top of that, he was on the verge of wetting his pants.

"Oh, no, no, no, don't start crying now, sweetheart. You wasn't boohooing when y'all collected that cash and placed that bomb in my nephew's coffin," Zekey told Miles. "Nah, y'all were as happy as a fag with a bag fulla dicks then." He tucked his gun and grabbed a black leather bag filled with dead white men. This was Miles and Ty's payment for making sure the explosive was placed inside the bottom of the coffin.

Zekey unzipped the leather bag and dumped its contents on Miles. Stack after stack of blue-face one-hundred-dollar bills rained down on him and even deflected off his head. Once Zekey had emptied the bag, he flung it aside and upped his gun again.

"Mmmmmm!" Miles' eyes exploded open, and he screamed behind the duct tape over his mouth. He pleaded for his life to be spared, but no one knew what he was actually saying.

"The money's all yours, big dog. I hope it's enough to buy your way outta Hell!" Zekey told him before he put six in his face. Miles fell on his side, dead, and blood poured out of his head, saturating the dirt. Zekey reloaded his gun and walked up on Wilt, giving him the business.

Poc, poc, poc, poc, poc, poc, poc!

That hot shit opened up his face and chest like a surgeon. He fell over on his side, twitching, with blood pouring out of his fatal wounds. Zekey stood over him and finished the job. He let him have the rest of his magazine and then flung his gun aside. It lay in the tall grass smoking.

Zekey kneeled down to the blood that had pooled underneath Wilt. He motioned every one over as he pressed his hand into the blood.

"We're gonna make a pact and we're gonna seal it in blood," Zekey told them. "Y'all press y'all hands down in this blood like I did." He stood upright with his dripping hand held at his side. Quan tucked her gun at the small of her back and pressed her hand down into the blood. Lil' Saint and Hellraiser exchanged glances, wondering what they should do. Hellraiser shrugged, kneeled down, and pressed his hand into the blood. Lil' Saint came behind him and did the same.

"Now what do we do?" Lil' Saint asked Zekey.

"Pile your hands on top of mine," Zekey told them. First came Quan's bloody hand, Lil' Saint's bloody hand, and then, finally, Hellraiser's. "Okay, now, y'all repeat after me."

"I solemnly swear to exact revenge on those involved in the attack on KiMani and Arnez, even if accomplishing my mission leads to my death or my life-long incarceration," they said altogether.

After the blood pact, they wiped the blood from their hands, got in their vehicles, and left the field.

Zekey was able to find out through Ty that a big African man had dropped a $100,000 bag on the niggaz he'd whacked to place the bomb in Arnez's coffin. They weren't one hundred percent about it, but they were positive that the African man was one of Assassin's hittaz.

***

Assassin sat in his father's big, black, leather executive office chair, staring at a portrait of them at the beach when he was seven years old. He clicked the safety on and off his gun like it was an uncontrollable habit. Suddenly, he threw the portrait hard as fuck against the wall and shattered its glass. Its twinkling shards rained down upon the carpeted floor behind the ruined portrait.

"Fuck that nigga, may he rest in shit," Assassin said of his father. He took a deep breath and sank down in the big chair. Using the tips of his sneakers, he turned his chair from left to right, playing like a bored child. He glanced at his timepiece, wondering what was taking Abrafo so long to holla at him. He'd called for his presence half an hour ago, and he'd neglected to show his face.

Assassin ran his hand down his face and took in his surroundings. The study was spacious. Its shelves were lined with books, medieval times-era weapons hung on the wall, a 42-inch flat screen was mounted over the fireplace, and knights in full metal body armor holding huge swords stood upright in all four corners of the room. The smell of funky armpits and ass crack lingered in the air, thanks to the Kush Assassin had blown an hour prior.

Knock, knock, knock, knock!

Assassin turned towards the door and sat his gun on the desk top. He then pressed a red button that was underneath the edge of the desk. There was a faint buzzing and the metallic click of a lock coming undone. Right after, Abrafo cracked the door open and peered inside at Assassin.

"You wanted to have a word with me?" Abrafo asked.

"Yeah, where the fuck you been all this time?" Assassin replied.

"I was using the bathroom. My stomach has been giving me trouble."

"That's all that weird ass Ghanaian food yo' ass been eating," he told him honestly. "I told you to lay off that shit."

Abrafo waved him off. He wasn't trying to hear all that shit. He loved his wife's cooking. It reminded him of home, so there wasn't any way in hell he was going to give it up. Besides, he was sure it wasn't the cultural food he'd eaten that had him shitting like a goose. He was positive it was the strawberry Nestle Quik milk he'd consumed earlier. He was lactose intolerant, but he'd seen so many commercials about the delicious beverage he tried it anyway. Big mistake!

"What was it that you wanted to see me about?" Abrafo asked, wanting to get right down to business.

"Come inside and have a seat," Assassin replied and waved him inside.

After Abrafo shut the door behind him, he pulled up a chair to the desk and sat down. His forehead was wrinkled with lines, wondering what Assassin wanted to talk to him about.

"How long have we known each other, big dog?" Assassin asked.

"I'd say, uh, about four and a half to five years," Abrafo replied. He couldn't help wondering what he was getting at.

"That's right. Me and my nigga, Papoose, good rest his soul, were just teenagers when we first met chu," Assassin said, recalling the day he'd met the foreign assassin. Back then, Abrafo was a vagabond drifting from city to city, brawling with anyone willing to put money on the line to see him up against their best fighter. Assassin didn't know what it was, but something told him to bet all he had on the big African. He and Papoose did just that, and they walked away winners. Over time, the boys developed somewhat of a friendship with Abrafo. They learned that he was a highly trained killa where he was from in the Motherland.

Assassin thought he'd be a great addition to his father's organization, so he introduced him to Hitt-Man. Although Abrafo was working for Assassin's old man, he'd pledged his undying loyalty to him. It was because of him that he was able to make himself a nice living and get out of the gutter. On top of that, he was able to get the love of his life, Tulip, over into the United States on a K-1 visa. They had gotten engaged shortly thereafter and had been living in holy matrimony ever since.

"Yes. I'll never forget that day. It's 'cause of you my life has changed for the better," Abrafo admitted. "I'll forever be indebted to you, thank you."

"You're welcome, big dog."

"Now, what is it you wanted to discuss with me?"

"Shit is getting pretty hot out here, my nigga. The day may come when niggaz slump me," Assassin said in all honesty, with his fingers interlocked in his lap. "I can't let the niggaz that body me have the last laugh. With that being said, I'd like to give you a hunnit geez up front to blow that nigga KiMani's brains out should his people lay me down." He picked up the silver briefcase from behind his desk, sat it on the desk top, popped its locks, and opened its lid. He spun the briefcase around to Abrafo and let him see all the dead presidents lying before him. Each and every stack of the money was secured by a rubber band. "You'll get another hunnit geez once you splash his ass. How do you love that, my nigga?" Assassin asked, as he took the time to light up his half-smoked blunt and blew smoke up at the ceiling.

Abrafo grabbed one of the stacks of money out of the briefcase. He inhaled its scent, licked his thumb, and dragged it across the top of the stack of bills. The blue face dollars made a rapid shuffling sound as his thumb came into contact with them. He loved money! Money made the world go round, and you could purchase anything within your wildest dreams with it.

"As much as I'd like to take this money, I can't," Abrafo told him, and tossed the stack upon the others inside the briefcase. He then sat back in his chair and interlocked his fingers in his lap.

Assassin frowned when he did this. One hundred thousand dollars was a nice bag to drop in a nigga's lap, especially someone like Abrafo, who'd came from one of the poorest parts of Ghana.

"What, bro? It's notta 'nough or something?" Assassin asked with concern in his voice as he sat up in his chair.

"That's more than enough, but I wouldn't feel right taking upfront money from you," Abrafo admitted. "I'd rather get the entire lump sum once I've completed the task you've assigned to me."

Assassin nodded and massaged his chin, thinking about what Abrafo had said while smoke rose from the ember of his blunt. "I respect that." He tapped his fist to his chest. "I'll tell you what, though, Blood, we're gonna play it like this." He switched hands with the bleezy, took out a blank business card, and jotted down the information he wanted him to have. Abrafo took the card from him and looked it over. "That's my attorney, Rick Gold. If I get murdered out here by these niggaz, God forbid"—he knocked on the desk top—"you knock KiMani's wig off and collect your ends. My guy's already been instructed to give you 100k that I've already hit his hand with. But I'ma drop this bag on 'em and you'll be picking up twice as much once the job's done." He took a pull from his blunt again, blew smoke, and dumped grayish-black ashes into the ashtray on the desk top. "I'd like you to go holla at Rick so he'll be familiar with you, should you have to activate your Kill Switch on my behalf."

Abrafo nodded understandingly and thumped the card with his fingers. He then pocketed the card, stood upright, and touched fists with Assassin.

"I'm going to go home now... I mean, unless you want me stay a while longer," Abrafo said.

"Nah, it's all good. I've got plenty of hittaz on deck," Assassin assured him. Abrafo nodded and continued out of the door.

"Baby, where are you? Dinner's ready!" Niqua came over the speaker of the intercom.

Assassin dabbed out his blunt inside the ashtray and hopped up from his chair. He blew smoke out of his nose as he walked over to the intercom beside the door. He held the button down before speaking into its receiver.

"Where you at, lil' mama?" Assassin asked and listened for her response.

"In our bedroom."

"I'll be there inna sec," he replied, killed the lights in the study, and walked out of the door.

***

"I'm telling you, babe, once we move these thousand birds, I'm gon' be straight," Assassin assured Niqua from where he was sitting across from her. "I'm gon' make these niggaz out here bow down and kiss the ring." He stuck out his pinky ring. It was big and glittering with all the colors of the rainbow.

"You mean once we move these thousand birds *we're* gon' be straight," Niqua corrected him with a smile as she poured them both glasses of Ace of Spades. They were sitting at a push-cart table with a white tablecloth draped over it. Their plates consisted of lobster tails, medium rare T-bone steaks, loaded mashed potatoes, mixed vegetables, and garlic breadsticks. A bucket full of ice cubes sat aside with cool vapors rising from it. The golden Ace of Spades bottle was wedged in the bucket of ice at one point.

"My fault, mamas, once we move these thousand birds *we're* gon' be straight," Assassin corrected himself with a grin.

Nah, I said it right the first time, bitch! Now that you've introduced me to the plug, it's on. I don't need yo' old ass no more, so I'ma knock you off and rule this whole shit by myself, Assassin thought with a grin while massaging his chin.

"What chu smiling about?" Niqua asked curiously. She passed him a glass of bubbly and kept the other for herself.

"Nothing, really, I'm just excited about that deal we just closed," Assassin lied smoothly. "We can stop fucking with trap houses and just start hitting the clientele with weight." He took a sip of champagne. "Warring with these niggaz over corners is for the fucking birds. I'm tryna move on to bigger and better things. You feel me?"

"Most definitely." Niqua nodded before taking a sip of champagne. "I guess now you're gonna drop this lil' beef you have with Hellraiser and them."

Assassin's face twisted in anger. "Fuck no! I'm squashing all them niggaz," he assured her. "I've gotta destroy and I've gotta destroy completely. I don't want any one of them niggaz to rise from the ashes and come looking to take my head."

Niqua nodded understandingly. She lay back in her chair and watched Assassin tear into his steak. He dipped his lobster tail into the hot butter and took a bite of it. He was in the middle of munching when he noticed Niqua wasn't eating. She was just sipping bubbly and looking at him with sparkling eyes.

"You're not hungry?" Assassin asked her with the sway of his fork.

"For this? Nope," Niqua said, swallowing the last of her champagne. She then picked up the Ace of Spades bottle. "What I want isn't on the menu, lil' daddy." Shorty tilted the golden bottle upward and drank from it thirstily, her throat moving up and down.

"Well, what do you want?" Assassin asked while holding the other half of lobster pinched between his thumb and finger.

"I want some dick," Niqua replied with a no-nonsense attitude.

"Say no more," Assassin said, eating the other half of the lobster tail, and sprung to his feet. He pulled his shirt over his head and flung it aside. Meanwhile, Niqua had stripped down to her bra and thong and kicked her pile of clothes aside. She then pulled Assassin into her and kissed him hard and lustfully. She lowered him down to his knees and he looked up at her like she was a goddess. Lifting her feet, she twiddled her pretty toes and then stuck her foot inside of his mouth. He grabbed her by her heel and sucked on her foot, moaning with his eyes closed. He sucked on her foot like it was a Fudge Popsicle, licked between her toes, and then up the arch of her foot. She popped her breasts out of her bra one at a time. They dropped then sprung back up, sitting up nicely with their nipples erect like pacifiers. Niqua drank from the golden Ace of Spades bottle thirstily and spilled a little down her chin. She wiped her dripping mouth and looked down at Assassin sucking on the ball of her foot. As he handled his business, he pulled his thick, vein-riddled dick from his opened zipper and stroked it up and down. His shit grew longer and harder in his hand.

"Mmmmmummmmm," Assassin moaned and slobbered on Niqua's foot while holding it by her ankle. Sucking on her foot aroused him beyond belief and made his piece incredibly hard. Niqua was older than him, but her body was banging. Shorty took damn good care of herself, and it showed. She could give half the bitchez her age a run for their money, and he was sure of that.

Assassin looked Niqua right in her eyes as he licked her foot straight up and started sucking on her foot again. She took the golden bottle to the head again, and then poured some of its contents down her thigh. The sudsy alcohol flowed down her thigh, her leg, over her foot, and into Assassin's mouth. He drunk from her foot, kissed it, and stood upright. Niqua grasped his neck and spat the champagne from her mouth into his. He spat it back into hers. She swallowed it, wrapped her arms around his neck, and tongued him down. Their eyes were closed as they turned their heads this and that way, kissing.

Niqua dropped the Ace of Spades bottle and some of the champagne spilled onto the carpet. Assassin walked her back towards the bed while kissing her and unhooking her bra. He tossed her bra aside, kicked off his jeans, and helped her take off her thong. He went back to kissing her, gripping her buttocks and rubbing all over them. His dick was poking at her flat stomach. White clear-like semen oozed out of his peehole and hung daringly from his mushroom tip. His piece was pulsating and so were the veins covering its shaft.

"On Blood gang, you thick as fuck, ma," Assassin said as he bit down on his bottom lip and groped her breasts. He flicked her nipples with the tip of his tongue and sucked on each one passionately. She gasped and threw back her head. Hissing, she closed her eyes and licked her lips. Her soft hands rubbed up and down his neck and back as he sucked her luscious titties. The combination of his warm, wet mouth and strong hands had her essence running between her legs. Her clit became rigid, and her pussy jumped like it was having muscle spasms. He had her really riled up. She wanted to be fucked—nah, she *needed* to be fucked!

Tranay Adams

Chapter Nine

"Damn, lil' daddy, I want chu—I—I want chu—in the—in the worst way," Niqua said with her eyes closed while running her fingers through his dread locs. His sensual moaning made her twat flow freely with more of her essence. The young nigga was driving her insane, and she wanted him deep up in her again. They hadn't even been fucking around that long. In fact, he had only smashed her twice before now, and she already thought she was in love with him. "I want—I want chu to—to fuck me—pleeease—fuck me right—right now."

Assassin ignored Niqua's sexual wants while continuing to grope and devour her tits. He grabbed a fistful of her hair and yanked her head back, making her groan. His tongue slowly traveled up her throat. He gently bit her under her chin, sucked on her bottom lip, and kissed her mouth. They made out while her hands played in his dread locs. She pulled back from kissing him, and he could see his reflection in her pupils. Her eyes told him she was craving him, and her pussy told him it was desperate to be filled by him.

"Daddy, I want chu to—uh!" Niqua yelled as Assassin aggressively grabbed her by the neck and squeezed it. He looked at her with his face scrunched and clenched jaws. As he held her about the neck with one hand, he kicked her legs apart and rubbed on her juicy clitoris with his other hand. She moaned loudly, and her entire body shook. She frowned, and her mouth hung open.

"Bitch, you don't dictate to me when you get some of this dick. I'm the head nigga in charge!" Assassin told her. His hot champagne breath blowing into her face and his gangsta demeanor had her extremely turned on. Her eyes rolled to their whites, and she went on shaking more intensely. "You hear me? Huh? You hear what the fuck I'm saying to you?" He shook her neck violently, and it excited her more.

"Gaaggg—yes—yes—choke me—choke me harder—" Niqua urged him. He did exactly that, and veins sprouted over her forehead and neck. She smacked his hand away from clit and rubbed her clit super-fast. The friction built up along with her orgasm. Her veins became more pronounced, and her chocolate skin became flushed. "Aaaaaaaah! Shiiiiiiiiit, niggaaaaaa!"

Niqua's pussy erupted and created its own tsunami below her. Assassin lowered her to the floor and kissed her sloppily while still gripping her neck. The entire time, she was still shaking and drenching the carpet.

"Yeah, stay there, stay right there, you fine mothafucka you," Assassin commanded her. He went through the pockets of his jeans until he found a red band. Pulling as many of the dread locs back into a ponytail as he could, he then tangled the band around it. He walked back over to Niqua, who was licking her tongue at him and manipulating that small flap of meat between her legs. She frowned, and her body tensed up. It then shook faster and faster, and she erupted again, saturating the surface below her.

"Oh, horny ass bitch!" Assassin said as he approached, stroking his rock-hard meat. He stood over her and smacked the shit out of her. Her head whipped around, and her braids flew. She looked back around at him excitedly with redness stinging her cheek. She loved that shit! The combination of pain and pleasure really got her ass going. Assassin could tell by the look in her eyes, so he smacked her again and again. Each time was harder than the last and resonated throughout the bedroom. Niqua's eyes fluttered as she toyed with her nipples. Once again, her ass shook and erupted again.

Assassin had her old ass open like a can of paint. He listened to her and studied her to learn everything she wanted and desired in the bedroom. In doing so, he opened doors of pleasure for her she didn't even know existed.

Assassin crawled up on the end of the bed. He planted his feet upon the mattress to give himself balance, and aimed his crinkle down at Niqua's face. He pumped his dick as she licked his asshole and sucked on his taint (the area between his nutsack and butt hole). He frowned with his eyes closed and his mouth open. He cussed under his breath and pumped his dick harder and faster. Him getting his poop shooter eaten out felt incredible to him.

Although he'd gotten it done to him before, it was never done by an experienced woman. Niqua knew exactly what she was doing, unlike the younger girls he'd been with. They'd just eaten his ass because he demanded it. The shit wasn't a labor of love. With Niqua, on the other hand, it was different. She ate his butt with care and passion. It was like she was making love to it with her mouth.

"Aaaaaah—aaaaaahhh—yeah, yeah, eat my shit!" Assassin said with a scrunched face, pumping his dick so hard the veins in his temple puffed up. "Eat my—eat my ass—uhhh, shit, that feels…that feels good. Mmmmm!"

The tantalizing sensation was so great to Assassin, he started moving his asshole back and forth across Niqua's tongue. Her warm, wet mouth had his peehole oozing with a clear fluid and his booty hole winking at her. Niqua continued to pleasure his brown eye while rubbing her clit with one hand and making sexual noises.

"Aaaaah! Shiiiit!" Assassin threw his head back and gritted. He was pumping his shit so fast his hand turned into a blur. "Yeah, that's it! Right there, mamas, right there!" he told her while she was sucking on his taint again. His piece swelled to capacity, becoming harder and harder. "Ah, you fucking dirty black bitch! Ooooooh!!"

Assassin's eyes exploded open as he shot white string after white string out of his dick head. He collapsed on the bed, breathing hard, with his back rising and falling. Niqua looked down at her pussy as she continued to please herself. She made a hideous face, and then she erupted again. She stretched her legs in front of her and laid her head back against the mattress. Her breasts rose and fell as she breathed. All of those orgasms had left her beat.

"Come on. Climb up on this bed and ride this dick, cowgirl," Assassin ordered, as he lay flat on his back, patting the bed while stroking his piece. His meat was standing long and strong. It was as hard as a brick of solid gold, and its swollen head was thumping like it had a heartbeat.

Niqua took a breath and climbed up on wobbly legs. She crawled onto the bed and mounted Assassin like a Ducati sport. Reaching behind her, she grabbed his penis and lowered herself upon it. Its girth expanded her pussy hole and filled her up to capacity.

"Fuuuuuck," Assassin and Niqua said in unison under their breaths. She felt his package deep within her treasure and he felt the 98 degrees of heat between her legs. Assassin held her waist as she gyrated her hips and made him hit spots within her that drove her wild. Niqua moaned and groaned while making interchangeable fuck faces. Shorty licked her top row of teeth and placed her hands down on Assassin's pecs, speeding up her pace. Her hips moved to an imaginary beat while her pussy oozed its natural nectar.

"Uh, uh, uh, I'm—I'm cuming—I'm cuming—" Niqua announced with a scrunched face while sinking her acrylic nails into Assassin's pecs and making blood appear. His face balled up and his top lip peeled back in a sneer. That shit hurt, but the pussy was great! He bit down on his bottom lip to combat the burning in his chest, and clutched her waist tighter. The meat there spilled between his fingers. He saw the euphoric look on her face as well as the sweat peppered on her forehead. Her mouth was quivering, and her titties were bouncing up and down as she moved in a circular motion. A devilish smile formed on his lips as he watched her enjoy herself.

Yeahhh, mamas, gon' and get yours, 'cause as soon as we're done, I'ma knock yo' pretty lil' head off yo' shoulders. I just had to tap this ass just one last time, Assassin thought and licked his lips while still smiling devilishly.

Smack!

Assassin swatted Niqua's left buttock, and she moaned and whimpered.

Smack!

Assassin swatted her right buttock. This time she moaned, whimpered, and shivered.

Assassin pulled her down onto him. He held her down with one hand across her back and the other around her waist. He bent his knees upward and planted his feet firmly in the bed for balance. He then started jack-hammering her hard, deep, and fast. She cried out and grasped the sheets in both her hands. Her pussy was farting and oozing white foam. The faster he went, the louder she moaned. Shorty started saying his name over and over again.

"Assassin—ouuuuu—Assassin—daddy—that's the spot—that's—that's the—" Niqua hollered out as she got her shit pushed in. Shorty exploded with another tsunami. She drenched Assassin's hairy thighs and dangling nutsack. She then went limp in his arms while he kept jack-hammering her, causing her to squirt more and more.

Assassin made a monstrous ass face while holding Niqua tighter and hammering her like a mad man. He could feel his dick swelling with his babies and demanding to be set free.

"Aaah—aaah, fuck! Here I cum! Grrrr, here I mothafucking cum! Aaaaah!" Assassin yelled as he erupted inside of her sopping pussy. A relieved expression was plastered across his face as he kept pumping deep inside of her. Hot spurts shot out of his peehole and splashed against her internal pink walls. She whimpered and frowned while quivering again. The feeling of him splashing against her walls made her orgasm again. Still, Assassin kept hammering into her until he'd given her all he had. He then fell flat out and took a deep breath. His face and chest were peppered with sweat. The nigga looked like he'd maxed himself out at the gym or some shit.

"Damn, that was—that was—that was amazing, lil' daddy," Niqua told him as she kissed him all over his chest.

"Lil' daddy? Hmmph! Ain't shit lil' 'bout me," Assassin said between breaths, as he was breathing heavily.

Niqua looked up from kissing on him and grinned at him. "I'm sorry, baby, *Big* Daddy."

"That's right. Put some respect on my shit," Assassin told her with a dead serious ass face.

"Whatever," Niqua said, smacking her lips and playfully hitting him. She went back to kissing on his chest when they heard automatic gunfire coming from outside the mansion. Assassin, wide eyed, popped up from the bed and shoved Niqua off him. She fell to the floor with a thud and scrambled back up on her bare feet. Shorty ran to the other side of the bed and grabbed a device as big as a PSP. It was to the surveillance cameras that monitored outside and inside the mansion. When she looked at the screen, she could see the killaz they'd hired blasting at a van. She showed it to Assassin. He couldn't believe what he was watching.

"Shiiiit, it's Hellraiser! That's who it's gotta be!" Assassin told her and tossed the device on the bed.

Knock, knock, knock!

"Niggaz broke through the gates! We're under attack!" one of the killaz said from outside the bedroom door.

"Y'all hold it down out there. Make sure no one makes it up here!" Niqua told them as she put her hair up in a bun and slipped her thong back up on her.

"We got chu, queen! Come on, man, she wants up to post up," Niqua and Assassin overheard the killa tell another.

Niqua darted towards the huge walk-in closet with Assassin on her heels, zipping up his jeans and buckling his belt. He slipped his shirt over his head and stuck his arms through its sleeves as he crossed the threshold into the walk-in closet behind her.

Ka-Boom!

The explosion from the outside rocked the entire mansion and knocked off Niqua and Assassin's equilibrium. Assassin fell to the carpeted floor but quickly scrambled back up on his sneakers. He saw Niqua reach beyond a rack of men's suits and pull what he gathered was a lever, downward. The sound of something large and metallic unlocking resonated inside of the closet. Then the space that most of her clothes and some of her shoes occupied made a 180 turn. On the opposite side, there were bulletproof vests, combat boots, knives, pistols, assault rifles, ammunition, and army fatigues, among other things.

"Come on. We've gotta hurry up," Niqua said as she grabbed a bulletproof vest and tossed Assassin one. As he began strapping his vest on, she removed another to strap onto herself. They put on the army fatigues and sheathed knives on their waistlines. Niqua snatched an M-16 assault rifle from a row of others. She loaded it up, chambered a round into it, and turned around to Assassin. His eyes widened and his mouth hung open. He lifted his hands up, surrendering. He never expected to be at her mercy, but the tables had turned on his ass. "What the fuck are you doing?" she asked him with furrowed brows.

"I thought chu were about to—"

"Kill you? Don't be silly," Niqua told him with a smirk. "You know how to work one of these, or would you prefer a pistol?"

"Nah, I can rock with that," Assassin assured her as he lowered his hands. He was thankful she hadn't blown his ass away.

"Good," Niqua said, walking over to him and kissing him. She passed him the assault rifle and grabbed another for herself.

"What's that door lead to?" Assassin asked while pointing at a door half the size of a closet. It was in between two shelves that were lined neatly with women's shoes. Niqua looked over her shoulder at the door he was referring to. At this time, the automatic gunfire could be heard coming from the outside along with the screams and hollers of men.

"That door leads to every room inside of this place, even the roof," Niqua told him, then loaded and cocked her assault rifle. She loaded a couple banana clips inside the pockets of her tactical vest and ran towards the entrance of the walk-in closet. She nudged Assassin as she ran past him so he would follow her.

Niqua unlocked the bedroom door. She was about to pull it open when she realized she didn't hear Assassin behind her. She whipped around, and he was gone. It was like he'd vanished. Her forehead creased, wondering where the hell he'd disappeared to.

"Assassin? Assassin! Assassiiiin!" Niqua called his name louder and louder. When she didn't get a response, she took a breath and snatched open the door. Entering the hallway, she saw and heard the killaz that were at her bedroom door earlier busting at the opps.

***

Since Assassin had been feuding with Hellraiser and them, he beefed up his home security system and hired an army of killaz to guard his father's estate. He had niggaz with assault rifles patrolling the grounds of the mansion twenty-four-seven. They had strict instructions to chop down anything and anyone who entered the perimeter that didn't belong. The days and nights had been long and boring since the killaz had been on duty, but tonight, all of that was about to change.

"Yo, what the fuck is that coming up?" one of the killaz on the rooftop asked, looking through his high-tech binoculars.

"Lemme see," the killa standing beside him said, taking the binoculars and giving him his assault rifle. He looked through them and saw something flying at the gates of the mansion like a missile. He couldn't quite see it, so he adjusted the dial to see with clarity. Once the visual came into focus, he saw that he was actually seeing a big ass van, with a crash bar on its grill. "Oh, shit, we're under attack!" He handed the binoculars back to the other killa and took his assault rifle from him.

The killa who had taken the binoculars back had quickly contacted the other killaz on deck. He let the other men know what was up, and they all took up their positions to defend the mansion. *Ba-Booooom!* The van burst through the gates of the mansion and the killaz immediately opened up on it. All the gunfire made it sound like Chinese New Year. What looked like a million holes appeared over the speeding van and made it look like Swiss cheese. No matter how many bullets were pumped into the vehicle, it kept on coming until it eventually slammed into the bottom steps. The automatic gunfire stopped. The night became still and silent, but the crickets were still making noise in the grass.

Three ropes were tossed off the rooftop of the mansion, one after the other. Then killaz started sliding down them with ease.

As they were coming down the ropes, the killaz on the grounds, pointing their assault rifles at the van, cautiously moved in on it. The killa leading the pack approached the driver's door of the vehicle. The window had a cobwebbed crack in it, so he used the butt of his assault rifle to shatter its glass. He knocked out the jabbed broken glass sticking up from the windowsill and then opened the driver's side door from the inside. The other killaz surrounding the van with their assault rifles at it stood by antsy and ready to kill.

The lead killa snatched open the door. He was surprised he didn't see anyone inside the van. However, he did see a hunting knife sticking up from the gas pedal, which had nailed it to the floor. This was how the van was able to drive forward.

"What's up, nigga? Who's in there?" one of the killaz asked.

"No one! They rigged this bitch to drive itself!" the lead killa announced. He then snatched the knife from out of the gas pedal. *Sniiiiikt!* He turned around, holding up the knife for the others to see. "I don't know what the meaning of this shit was unless it wassa…" He dropped the knife and ducked back inside of the van. He looked underneath the driver's seat and saw the timer on an explosive. It had two seconds on it. "Decoy."

The killa'z eyes widened fearfully, and then the big bang came—*Ka-Boooom!* The explosion was loud and furious. Its impact disintegrated many of the killaz and sent many others high up into the air. Severed body parts along with droplets of blood rained down on the lawn. The wreckage of the van burned while the men who were wounded moaned in pain.

The ground rumbled as something enormous and heavy trampled through the entrance of the estate. When the remaining killaz looked up, they saw an armored Brink's truck coming at them. They upped their assault rifles and opened fire on it. *Ping, ping, ting, zing, king, ring!* Sparks flew off the hard-metal truck as bullets deflected off of it. No matter how many shots they sent at the damn thing, it just kept on coming at them. A couple of them dove out of the path of the Brink's truck, but it managed to crush two of them.

"Gaaaaaah!"

"Aaaaaaaah!"

The killaz screamed horrifically as the heavy metal truck crushed their bodies. Their bones crackled and popped underneath the 55,000 pounds of hulking machinery. The slots on all sides of the truck opened, and assault rifles emerged out of them. Fire flickered from the assault rifles and knocked some of the killaz off their feet. They made ugly faces as the bullets chopped them down. They lay where they were with their eyes and mouths stuck open and their blood saturating the lawn. The assault rifles wafted with smoke as they lingered out of the slots. Abruptly, they were snatched back inside of the Brink's truck.

The back doors of the truck unlocked and swung outward. One by one, Hellraiser, Lil' Saint, Quan, and Zekey jumped down on the lawn. They were wearing bulletproof vests and toting assault rifles. Hellraiser made sure everyone was accounted for and motioned for them to follow him. They charged up the steps of the mansion, keeping a close eye on their surroundings. Once they made it up to the double doors of the mansion, Hellraiser sprayed the door locks and then kicked them open. As soon as they ran in over the threshold, a couple of killaz ran up to the guard rail of the balcony and pointed their assault rifles down at them.

Buratatatatatatatatat!

Buratatatatatatatatat!

The killaz sprayed down at Da Crew, and the sound of automatic gunfire echoed throughout the mansion. Their bullets broke up the Italian-imported flooring, shattered vases, knocked big portraits off the walls, and turned the front doors into cheese graters. Da Crew held their assault rifles low as they scattered like roaches to avoid getting chopped down. They took cover behind furniture and statues while Hellraiser tried to figure out what move they should make next.

"Hold your fire!" Niqua said from behind the killaz as they held their smoking assault rifles. The killaz lowered their assault rifles and parted to make space for their boss. Niqua, wearing a bulletproof vest, strolled up to the guard rail with an M-16 assault

124

rifle. Her hair was pulled back and pinned up in a bun, and she was wearing war paint on her face.

Hellraiser frowned upon hearing Niqua's voice. She sounded familiar to him, but he couldn't quite put his finger on where he knew her from.

"Treymaine! Treymaine James, I know you're down there," Niqua said with a wicked smile. "Long time no see—baby daddy!"

"Shaniqua?" Hellraiser said with a gasp and his eyes widened.

"Shocking, isn't it? You thought a bitch was dead, but I'm alive and in the flesh!" Niqua told him.

Lil' Saint looked at Hellraiser with confusion in his eyes. Hellraiser, knowing what was on his mind, shrugged. He didn't know how to explain his son's mother's sudden resurrection from the dead.

"I'd been fucking Hitt-Man for quite some time, probably 'bout as long as you've been fucking that square-ass ho Lachaun," Shaniqua told him. "That nigga Hitt-Man's hatred for you stems from Caleb's love for you. He said that you were his favorite when he should have been. Can you fucking believe that shit? A grown-ass man jealous of the friendship between two other grown-ass men? If that's not the gayest shit I've ever heard in my life." She shook her head in disappointment. "I cannot believe I fell head over heels for a nigga like that."

Damn, I smoked Caleb with extreme prejudice thinking he'd killed my baby mama when he hadn't. That's fucked up! I'm sorry, my nigga, Caleb. I wish I could take it back, Hellraiser thought as he crossed himself in the sign of the Holy crucifix. *This bitch Shaniqua is deceitful, like that serpent in the Bible that tricked Eve into eating the forbidden fruit. What I don't understand is how in the fuck did she pull this shit off? I can't fathom the idea of her orchestrating all of this shit, especially with the hospital declaring her ass dead.*

"Anyway, he was sick of being under Caleb and wanted to be the man. He was gonna kill both of y'all, but I convinced 'em him to do otherwise with my soft ass," Niqua told him. "Why? 'Cause deep down inside, I was still madly in love witchu. So I came up with a plan to get both of y'all out the way. That day at cho lil' girlfriend's house, I had 'em drive by firing blanks at me. I taped the squibs they use in the movies onto my back and triggered them to explode once he'd gotten close enough."

"This bitch is cold with it, babe," Quan whispered to Zekey.

"I know. I can't even front," Zekey whispered back.

"The ambulance, the cops that showed up, the doctor at the hospital that came out and told you I didn't make it. They were all paid," Niqua said. "One thing I know about chu, Treymaine, you're one prideful, murdering bastard. I knew once you were convinced that Caleb sanctioned the hit that I was accidentally killed in, that you'd come looking for blood, and I was right. You killed Caleb, and Hitt-Man took over his operation. You got hit with fifteen years, and here we are now. Pretty clever, huh, baby daddy?" She smirked wickedly.

"What about our son, huh? What about him?" Hellraiser inquired. "You know the young nigga you laying up with is the reason behind 'em laying up in the hospital and his best friend being killed? Did you know that? Huh?"

"Nigga, I don't give a fuck about KiMani's lil' thug ass," Niqua admitted with a scowl. "I had 'em on the account of you. He wassa 'keep a nigga' baby." She made air quotations with her fingers. "I couldn't give a rat's ass if he lives or dies. That's yo' son, not mine!"

"That's fucked up. This bitch is heartless," Quan whispered to Zekey.

Zekey had a look on his face like, *Man, this broad is something else.*

Hearing Shaniqua speak like this made Hellraiser think back to when he first discovered she had been mentally and physically abusing KiMani. His eyebrows slanted, wrinkles formed around his nose, and he gritted so hard his teeth felt like they were going to break. Gripping his assault rifle as firmly as he could, he cautiously eased his head out from his hiding place and looked up at Shaniqua. She put on a little weight and had obviously gotten a boob job, but it was definitely her. He was sure of that.

"Well, you may not know this, but he's inna coma at the hospital! Before he went under, he gave me something to give you that he really wanted you to have!" Hellraiser yelled up to Shaniqua and signaled to his crew what move to make. They all nodded and took up their positions.

Niqua's forehead creased, wondering what her son could possibly want her to have. "What the fuck could he possibly wanna give me?"

"This!" Hellraiser yelled and swung out from his hiding place. He upped his assault rifle and chopped down one of the killaz standing beside Shaniqua. He screamed as his ass was painted bloody, and flipped over the guard rail. He fell awkwardly on his head and broke his neck. Shaniqua backed up down the hallway, spraying down at Da Crew. The killa left on the balcony was splattered by Quan, Zekey, and Lil' Saint's automatic gunfire. His blood splattered against the wall behind him, and he tumbled down the stairs quickly.

"We're gonna split up, y'all, Zekey and Lil' Saint, y'all together," Hellraiser whispered to them. "Queen," he looked to Quan. "Yo' ass is with me, we're gonna get this bitch and her nigga. Their asses are going down tonight. I put that on my—"

Ratatatatatatatatat!

Ratatatatatatatatat!

The spraying of assault rifles cut Hellraiser short. He, Zekey, Lil' Saint, and Quan exchanged fire with the killaz who'd appeared out of the hallway. Bullets were flying all around them, knocking the cotton out of the sofa and love seat. Holes appeared inside the hallway and on the outside of it. The killaz were about to move in to kill Da Crew, but the gun battle became too intense for them. One of the killaz caught one in his thigh, dropped his assault rifle, and howled in pain. He hurriedly limped away, holding his wound while his comrade laid down cover fire for him. Once his comrade, the other killa, was sure Zekey and Lil' Saint would be off their asses long enough for them to retreat, he ran off behind the killa that fled.

"Yo, me and Saint gon' go after these niggaz, you and wifey handle yo' baby mama," Zekey told Hellraiser.

"Alright, love, fool." Hellraiser dapped him up and they touched fists.

"Love, my nigga," Zekey replied.

Hellraiser dapped up and touched fists with Lil' Saint too. Zekey kissed Quan, told her to be careful, and took off running down the hallway with Lil' Saint by his side.

"Okay, queen, it's you and me," Hellraiser told Quan as they made their way up the stairs.

"That's what it is then, king," Quan said, dapping him up.

Once they made it up on the balcony, Hellraiser crept alongside the wall until he'd reached its corner. Easing his head out from where he was against the wall, he could see Shaniqua's shadow and hear her talking to someone over her cellphone. Hellraiser knew it was best to strike now while she was distracted. He pulled out a grenade and snatched out its ring. He waited a second and tossed it inside the hallway. The grenade deflected off the wall and tumbled down the corridor.

Chapter Ten

Zekey and Lil' Saint strategically moved down the corridor with their assault rifles leading the way. They checked room after room, looking for the killaz they'd shot it out with. Everything was gravely quiet until an eerie sound disturbed them. They swung their assault rifles around ready to fire, but they didn't see anyone at their rear. Zekey held up his hand, signaling for Lil' Saint to stay back while he checked to see what caused the disturbance. Lil' Saint nodded his understanding and stayed where he was with his assault rifle held low.

Zekey crept down the hallway cautiously with his eyes and ears open. He'd crossed a door to his left that one of the killaz had slowly opened, but he hadn't noticed it. The killa was creeping up behind Zekey with his assault rifle to lay his ass out. Lil' Saint's eyes widened when he saw the killa about to make his move. He went to lift his assault rifle and open fire, but was caught off guard with what happened next.

"Ooof!" Lil' Saint made a pained noise as he was tackled by the killa with the wounded leg. His assault rifle fired up at the ceiling, making debris fall and alerting Zekey in the process. Zekey whipped around with his assault rifle and was shocked to see the killa at his back. He went to pop his ass but found his weapon was empty. The dread loc-wearing killa smiled wickedly, displaying his mouthful of shiny gold teeth. The killa was about to split Zekey's wig, but the ex-convict proved to be quicker than he appeared. Swiftly, he kicked the killa's assault rifle out of his hand, and it flew back over his head. He slammed the butt of his weapon into his stomach and doubled him over. He followed up, whacking him in the jaw with it and then forcing him up against the wall. Zekey gritted as he forced his assault rifle against the dread-loc killa's windpipe. The sweaty-face killa made an ugly face and gagged, struggling to breathe. Thick, squiggly veins sprouted over his forehead and neck as he struggled with control over the assault rifle.

"Die, bitch-ass nigga! Die!" Zekey said hatefully, with beads of sweat oozing out of his forehead. He had the upper hand. The killa's strength was dwindling, and he was at Zekey's mercy.

"Fuck—grrrrrr—you!" the dread-loc killa shouted and kneed Zekey in the jewels. Zekey hollered out and grabbed his balls. The assault rifle dropped to the floor! The killa punched Zekey square in the face. He bounced off the wall and fell to the floor, holding himself. His eyes were squeezed shut and he was gritting in unbearable pain. The dread-loc killa smiled devilishly and slid his tongue over his top row of gold teeth. Pressing his hands against the wall, he went to work, kicking and stomping Zekey callously.

***

Lil' Saint and the killa, who was baldheaded, landed in the wash room. The fall had knocked the wind out of Lil' Saint, and his bumping the back of his head on the floor had him dizzy. The baldheaded killa saw that he was vulnerable and took full advantage of it. He grasped him tightly around his neck and punched him in the face repeatedly. He then slipped behind Lil' Saint, unbuckled his leather belt, and yanked it back against his neck. The bald killa scowled and clenched his jaws as he tightened the belt around his throat. Lil' Saint's eyeglasses hung crookedly on his face as he fought for his life. His eyes widened and watered, and his mouth was stuck open. Gagging, he tried to slip his fingers underneath the belt, but it was too tight around his neck. The veins in his forehead and neck threatened to burst while blood clots began to form in his eyes. The little man was dancing on the tight rope between life and death!

"Lil' mothafucka, you see God yet? Huh? You see 'em?" the baldhead killa asked through clenched teeth and sweat sliding down his face. The veins in his forehead and arms bulged as he applied more pressure to Lil' Saint's neck.

Lil' Saint was lightheaded, and he felt like he was on the verge of blacking out. He knew he had to do something fast, or he was going to be flying around in Heaven wearing a white gown. With that in mind, he placed his hands and boots firmly against the floor. He then dipped as low as he could and launched his head upward. His head struck the baldhead killa in his nose and drove its bone directly into his brain. He died upon impact, and his head fell back against the floor. Blood accumulated in his eyes like real tears and spilled down his face.

Lil' Saint, who was breathing hard and rubbing his aching neck, rolled off the baldhead killa's dead body. He lay on the floor trying to catch his breath, and thanking God Almighty above. Once he'd gathered himself, he picked up his assault rifle and used it as a crutch to get himself off the floor.

***

The dread-loc killa kicked Zekey in the side one last time. He wiped his sweaty forehead with his black T-shirt and made his way down the hallway. Zekey, still holding his jewels, looked up the hallway and saw the assault rifle he'd kicked out of dread locs' hands earlier. He knew he was going to get it to finish him off, and he wasn't about to let that happen. Combating the aching in his balls, Zekey pushed off the floor and charged towards dread loc like an angry bull. Dread loc, hearing the hurried footsteps behind him, went to turn around, but it was already too late. Zekey slammed into him, wrapped him in a bear hug, and lifted him high into the air. He then brought him down to the floor with as much force as he could muster.

Wooom!

Dread locs' face collided with the floor, busting his forehead, left eye, nose, and mouth. He lay where he was looking like he was planking. Blood was gushing out of his nostrils and mouth. The shit looked like a big ass bucket of red paint had tilted over. Wincing, Zekey limped down the hallway, holding his balls with one hand. When he picked up the assault rifle, he saw Lil' Saint coming out of the wash room. Zekey could tell from the looks of him he'd been in one hell of a fight, but he was glad his little ass was alive.

"Ol' boy whipped yo' ass." Zekey cracked a one-sided smile.

"Look who's talking," Lil' Saint replied with a one-sided smile as well.

"You good though?" Zekey asked him.

"Yeah, I'll be alright," Lil' Saint assured him, rubbing his neck. "Head's up." He nodded down the hallway.

Frowning, Zekey turned around, gripping his assault rifle, and saw dread locs shaking off his dizzy spell. He spat plasma on the floor and wiped the slimy ropes of blood from his chin. When he looked up to see Zekey charging at him with his assault rifle, he pulled a hunting knife from the sheath at the small of his back. He moved to rise from the floor to attack him, but the ex-convict was already up on him. Zekey cocked his foot back and launched it against dread locs' grill. The blow lifted the dread locs off the killa's shoulders and sent his hunting knife hurling backwards. The killa landed hard on his back, and his booted feet came down behind him.

Zekey beat dread locs' face with the butt of his assault rifle until it caved inward. He tossed the bloody weapon aside as Lil' Saint came to stand beside him.

"Come on. Let's go find Hell and my wife," Zekey told him.

***

Once her killaz started shooting it out with Da Crew, Niqua ran back into the hallway with her assault rifle and hit up her contact to carry out what they'd planned. She upped her assault rifle as she listened to her inside man's cell phone ringing in her Bluetooth. His cellular rang and rang, and she wondered why he hadn't answered.

Come on, come on! Pick up, pick up, pick up, Niqua thought.

"What up, sis?" a young nigga answered.

"Kyjuan, this is it, baby boy! Do it now, now!" Niqua hollered into the Bluetooth. "Holy shit!" Her eyes nearly leaped out of their sockets when a live grenade bounced off the wall and tumbled toward her. She took off running and then—*Ka-Boom!* The grenade exploded, sending shrapnel and fire everywhere. Its impact rocked the entire upstairs and slammed Niqua into the ceiling. She slammed back down onto the floor, fracturing her arm and breaking two of her ribs. She howled in pain, squeezing her eyes shut and clenching her teeth. She was hurting like a son of a bitch!

"Niqua, are you there? Are you there?" Kyjuan called out over the phone. "Fuck, Blood!"

***

Kyjuan sat his contraband cellphone aside on his bed. He pulled his shank from its hiding place and hopped off his bunk. He stepped up on his bunk where he found OG under the covers asleep. He drew the cover back and lifted his prison-fashioned blade to stab the old head in the neck. It was a pressure point there that was sure to make him bleed profusely until he died.

"What the fuck?" Kyjuan spat with his forehead furrowed in confusion. There was only the old man's pillow underneath the covers. He looked to the door then to the rest of the small cell. His forehead furrowed further when he didn't see him. He jumped down to the cool floor on his bare feet, with his back facing the bunks. A split second later, he felt two swift slices, and a burning sensation ripped through his Achilles tendons. Instantly, he lost his ability to stand and collapsed to his knees. A blood-curdling scream came from his mouth and made his uvula shake. Teary eyed, he turned to reach for his foot, but he couldn't quite reach it. However, he could see both his Achilles tendons had been severed and he was bleeding something awful.

OG slid from underneath the bottom bunk with a shank the size of a small sword. The shiny metal dripped with blood as the older man picked himself up from the floor. He looked older than usual and very sickly, but he still had a warrior's spirit. There was plenty of fight left in him. He coughed into his hand and looked into his palm. There was blood in it. He wiped it on his wife beater and decided to ignore it. He had a more pressing matter to attend to, like taking this fucker's life that had tried to kill him.

OG kicked Kyjuan so hard in his back, he pitched forward and slammed his face into the floor. The impact broke his nose, bloodied his mouth, and sent his shank spinning in circles across the surface. He lay there looking dizzy and moaning in pain.

"Lil' young-ass mothafucka, what chu thought? That I was gon' be an easy win 'cause I'm old and sickly? Huh?" OG hollered down at him. "Well, you've got it wrong, new school. I'm as deadly as I ever was behind this concrete and steel."

OG, being a man that had read over two thousand books during his incarceration, knew the functions of the human body like he knew the back of his hand. Using his shank, he sliced through the tendons and cartilage in Kyjuan's shoulders, elbows, and wrists that would render his arms useless. Kyjuan couldn't feel his arms, but he could feel the blood pouring from out of his wounds.

"Aye, man, aye, man—what the fuck—what the fuck did you do to me?" a wide-eyed Kyjuan asked in a panic-stricken voice. "Ughh!" He squeezed his eyes closed and gritted, feeling the old nigga stomp him in the middle of his back.

"Shut cho bitch-ass up, nigga!" OG spat furiously as he stood over him with his shank, which was still dripping blood. "You know the thang witchu wannabe gangstas of today? Huh?" He stomped him in his back again for not answering him.

"What, man? What?" Kyjuan hollered over and over again.

"You don't live by a code, and you think you know every fucking thang!" OG replied. "Not to mention you're sloppy. In fact, you're entirely too sloppy. You young boys get sent to take care of a couple of niggaz from the other side and you wind up shooting innocent bystanders. Ain't no respect in that! In my day, anyone who wasn't in the lifestyle was untouchable. And if you did make the mistake of harming them, then it was you who got dealt with."

"Heeeellllp, heeelllllp, heeelllp!" Kyjuan screamed louder and louder in hopes the corrections officers on duty would hear him.

"Youz a hardheaded nigga, I see," OG said with a frown, stomped his mouth four times, and then ground the side of his face into the floor. He'd successfully broken the young nigga's top and bottom jaw. Now he couldn't say much of shit. "Yeah, you fucked up. You really fucked up. You thought I didn't hear you that night when whomever it was told you to make sure you kill me if my boy killed them. That's what I meant by you young-ass niggaz being sloppy." He went into a coughing fit while holding his hand over his mouth. Looking at his palm, he saw it was bloody, but it didn't bother him. He already knew he was living on borrowed time. "This is the end of the road, Blood. You know what they say, you live by the sword then you die by the sword."

OG straddled Kyjuan's waist. The young man's body trembled fearfully. He stared out the corners of his eyes at OG and tried to plead for his life. Unfortunately for him, his broken jaw wouldn't allow him to say much. He could only say inaudible words that even he didn't understand. OG, using both hands, gripped his sword-like shank and brought it high over his head. With a grunt, he slammed it down with all his might. The knife went into the flesh of Kyjuan's back, through his ribcage, and stabbed into the floor. Although the youngsta had died instantly, the old head's stabbing didn't stop. He brought the shank down repeatedly into his back, blood dotting up his face and clothing.

"I'm an original gangsta killa, young boy! Ask about me when you make it down there!" OG said to Kyjuan's limp corpse as he continued to brutally assault it. "I done sent plenty were you've gone! You hear me, youngin'? Plenty!"

OG stabbed and stabbed Kyjuan until he was out of breath and the shank was standing up in his back like a flag. He picked up the young nigga's cellular and heard Hellraiser on the other end of it.

"Son? Yeah, I'm okay," OG told him, still panting, out of breath. He lay back on the bottom bunk. "I'm fine. Naw, that young punk is dead. I killed his ass." He harped up mucus and spat on Kyjuan. The loogey smacked him on his temple and ran down in his eye. "Look here, I don't know when I'ma see you again. The alarm just sounded and I can hear them boys stampeding to my cell. I just want you and the family to know I love y'all. Give my grandbabies a kiss for me, okay?"

"Okay, Pop. We love you too," Hellraiser replied.

OG threw the contraband cellphone aside and closed his eyes. He continued to listen to the blaring alarm and the stampeding corrections officers. A minute later, he could hear them unlocking the door of his cell. The next thing he knew, he was being roughly pulled off the bottom bunk, slammed to the floor beside Kyjuan's bloody body, and handcuffed.

***

The hallway was cloudy with smoke from the grenade exploding. Two silhouettes moved through the clouds with their firearms at their sides. The further they moved through the clouds, the more they became visible until Niqua could see them completely. Hellraiser and Quan stood over her. Her assault rifle was a foot away. She tried reaching for it, but Quan shot up her hand, splattering it across the floor. She hollered in agony and cradled what was left of her mutilated hand. Her face balled up as she gritted her teeth.

"That shit hurt, huh, bitch?" Quan asked as smoke rose from the barrel of her assault rifle. She looked at Hellraiser. "So this is your baby mama, huh?"

"Yeah." Hellraiser nodded as he mad dogged Niqua. "All this shit went down behind her. All of it." He took the Bluetooth from her ear and chopped it up with OG for a minute. Afterwards, he dropped the headset on the floor, stomping and mashing it out. Then he did the same thing to her cellular.

"Fuck y'all waiting for? I'm ready to die!" Niqua shouted hatefully and spat in Hellraiser's face. He frowned and wiped the sliding loogey from his cheek. "Kill me! Kill me, mothafuckaz! Kill—"

Blatatatataatat!

Niqua was cut short by a short burst of automatic gunfire to her chest that killed her instantly. Hellraiser and Quan lifted up their weapons and pointed them in the direction that the fire had come. As soon as they did, Quan caught fire, bumped into the wall, and slid down to the floor, leaving a bloody smear behind her. She sat on the floor wincing and holding her assault rifle at her side while Hellraiser disappeared at the corner of the corridor. He couldn't see the gunman who was trying to pick them off, thanks to the cloudy hall, so he had to be careful.

"Quan, you good?" Hellraiser asked from his hiding place, holding his assault rifle up at his shoulder.

"Y-yeah. I took two, but they went right through!" Quan looked to the bloody black holes in her shoulder and bicep. She scrunched her face and tightened her jaws from the excruciating pain in them.

"Good. But from what I can see, you're bleeding pretty bad," Hellraiser told her. "We're gonna have to put some pressure on those wounds before you bleed to death."

"Yeah, I know. I'm starting to feel—" Quan abruptly stopped talking.

"Starting to feel what?" Hellraiser asked with a frown. He didn't hear a response, so he called out to her again. "You're starting to feel what, Quan?" She still didn't say shit. "Yo, lil' mama, what's the deal? You okay?"

"She's okay, Pops, but if you don't toss your piece and come on out here, I'ma blow this fat bitch's head off," Assassin swore from inside the hallway. He was standing over Quan and holding an M-16 to her temple.

"Fuck this nigga, Trey. Don't—" Quan was cut short by Assassin kicking her in the temple. Her eyes rolled around like loose marbles and her head bobbled. She was dizzy and discombobulated.

"Shut cho fat ass up!" Assassin said, mad dogging Quan as he drew his foot back. "Yo, Pops, I'm not gon' tell you again!" he called out down the hallway to Hellraiser. As soon as he did, Hellraiser tossed his assault rifle into the corridor and stepped out with his hands up.

"Here I am, youngsta, right here," Hellraiser told him as he cautiously approached. Assassin smiled devilishly, seeing him at his mercy.

"You gotta be the biggest dummy I've ever laid eyes on," Assassin told him. "You really gon' risk your life behind this broad? She ain't even alla that." He stole a glance at Quan then focused his attention back on Hellraiser.

Hellraiser frowned, not liking how Quan was being referred to as a bitch. "She's a queen—a beautiful black queen," he stated firmly. "She's here risking her life tonight on my behalf. So, I'm willing to lay my life down for her. My loyalty runs deep."

"You OG niggaz and y'all codes. It's just too bad that code has left you at the mercy of my gun," Assassin told him as he took the M-16 from Quan's temple and pointed it at him. His forehead creased, seeing Hellraiser was staring past him and looking down at Niqua. "What? You feel some type of way 'cause I smoked yo' baby mama?"

"I thought she was your lady," Hellraiser replied, with a confused look.

Assassin glanced over his shoulder at Niqua's body and shrugged. "Old cougar fulfilled her purpose, so I putta ass down." He scowled at Hellraiser, and his nostrils flared. "But never mind alla that. I've had enough with the chit chat, it's time to die, nigga." He went to pull the trigger of his assault rifle, but Hellraiser's next words stopped him.

"I've seen the biggest cowards bust their gun and take a man's life," Hellraiser said. "That ain't 'bout nothing, though. That's easy," he assured him. "But when it comes down to them hands and that footwork, where you at with it? Do you have what it takes to bump with a G of my status?" Hellraiser looked into Assassin's eyes, and he could see that what he had said was getting to him. He was mulling the thoughts he'd projected to him over in his mind.

"Come on, youngin'. If you're anything like your old man, I know you can't turn down a fade."

"Alright, OG, you wanna dance with the kid?" Assassin asked as he tossed his M-16 aside. "Well, I hope you're up for it, 'cause it's not gonna be a walk in the park." He jumped up and down while wagging his hands and rolling his neck around on his shoulders.

"Oh, I'm definitely up for it, YG," Hellraiser stated as he removed his jacket and threw it aside. "The question is, 'are you?'" he asked, rolling his head around his shoulders and cracking his knuckles. He then stretched his arms and legs, making his bones make a crackling sound.

"It's only one way to find out, old timer." Assassin smiled devilishly, got into a fighting stance, and threw up his fists.

"Now we're talking," Hellraiser replied. He got into a fighting stance and threw up his fists as well.

Assassin gave Hellraiser a three-punch combination to the face and kicked him in the side of his knee, which left him kneeling. He kicked him in the stomach, he doubled over, and Assassin backhand punched him. Hellraiser dropped to his hands and knees. Bleeding at the mouth, he wiped away the blood with his fist. Assassin went to work, kicking him in his side while talking big shit.

"Old ass nigga, you ain't nothing but talk!" Assassin told him. "I must say, I am highly disappointed with your performance this evening. With all I've heard about chu, I expected so much more." He kicked Hellraiser in his side again, and he fell to the floor on his back. He then took the liberty to stomp his chest and his balls.

"Aaaaaah!" Hellraiser hollered with bulging eyes and gritted teeth, holding his precious jewels.

While all of this was going on, Quan was slowly starting to come to her senses, moaning due to her migraine headache. She saw blurry images of Hellraiser and Assassin at the middle of the hallway. Her vision was coming in and out of focus. She looked to her side and saw her assault rifle. She tried to pick it up, but her wounded arm wouldn't obey her mind's command.

"Uhhh, uhhh," Quan groaned in pain with a balled up face, trying to get her arm to budge.

Assassin gritted and stomped Hellraiser's body like a mad man. He didn't show him any mercy at all as he gave him a savage pummeling. Once he'd gotten tired of stomping his ass out, he took the time to wipe away the sweat peppered over his forehead and spat on the floor. He then looked down at Hellraiser like he was a pathetic piece of shit and shook his head in disappointment. When the older man tried to get up off the floor, Assassin rewarded him with another kick in his ribs, dropping him to the floor. He lay there holding his side and grimacing. The pain in his ribs told him that quite a few of them were fractured, but he knew he'd have to fight through it if he hoped to win.

Assassin threw his head back and gave a throaty laugh. He then looked around at his imaginary audience, repeating the words Killmonger did when he whipped T'Challa's ass in Wakanda. "Is this your king? Huh? Is this your king?"

Assassin grabbed Hellraiser by the front of his bulletproof vest and pulled him forward. Gritting, Hellraiser grabbed his wrist with both hands and kicked him hard as fuck in his balls. The veins in Assassin's forehead bulged, and his eyes nearly popped out of their sockets. A little vomit oozed out of the corner of his mouth. He was in so much agony, he couldn't mount a decent defense, and Hellraiser took advantage of this. Wrapping both his legs around his arm, he slammed him into the floor and broke his nose. Locking his legs firmly around his arm, he gripped him by his forearm and wrist tightly. Then, with all his might, he twisted his arm to his right and snapped that bitch! A loud popping sound echoed off the walls inside of the hallway.

"Aaaaaaaah!" Assassin screamed in excruciation, and his eyes opened so wide his pupils looked smaller than usual. Hellraiser released him and got up on his feet. He started kicking and stomping his bitch ass like he'd done him. He then cocked his boot back and launched it forward with thirty-pounds of pressure behind it. Upon impact, Assassin's mouth exploded in broken teeth and blood. His shit was leaking profusely, and he was spitting out fragments of broken teeth.

Hellraiser rose to his feet, swallowed a mouthful of blood, and frowned at the taste of copper. He held his side with one hand and motioned for Assassin to get up with the other.

"Get up, big man! Come on now, get up!" Hellraiser kicked Assassin in his side, and he grimaced. "I know you've got more fight in you than that!"

"Uhhh," Assassin said as he scrambled to his booted feet. His broken arm dangled limply at his side, completely useless, but he still had fire in him. "You're right, old man. I've got plenty of more fight in me." He spat blood aside and slimy ropes of it hung from his chin. Smiling devilishly, he pulled a bowie knife from the small of his back and held it before his eyes. It was two inches in width and seven inches in length. A gleam swept up the blade, and it twinkled at its curved tip.

Hellraiser became alert when he saw the knife come into play. A weapon as deadly as that was sure to cause some serious damage if it were to enter his body. With that in mind, he went on the defense to avoid the bowie knife at all cost. Assassin swung and thrust the knife at all of his most vital organs, but he managed to avoid it.

"Can't fuck with the old man from the shoulders, so you gotta pull knives and shit, huh?" Hellraiser said as he jumped back, moving from side to side to avoid the knife attack.

"Whatever gets the job done!" Assassin said with a grunt and thrust his knife forward. Hellraiser howled in pain as four inches of it went through his bulletproof vest and penetrated his torso. Assassin smiled devilishly once again and licked his bloody lips. He relished in the fact he'd caused his opponent great agony. He tried to pull his knife out of Hellraiser, but he kicked him in his chin and across his face. The blow whipped him around in a one hundred eighty-degree turn. He found Quan staring up at him from the floor with her assault rifle pointed at him.

"Stupid, mothafucka, no one ever told you notta bring a knife to a gunfight?" Quan asked as she pulled the trigger of her assault rifle. The automatic weapon vibrated in her gloved hand as it spat flames at Assassin. Hellraiser dove to the floor just as the rapid firing began, but his adversary wasn't so quick on his feet. Assassin got every bullet out of that rifle meant for his ass. He screamed as he spun around like a ballerina in ice skates and bullets tore his ass up. His blood dotted up the walls and the floor in the hallway. Once the assault rifle went still, he fell to his bloody demise. He hit the floor wide eyed with an open mouth. Blood poured out of every hole in his body and saturated the carpet.

Chapter Eleven

Quan took a deep breath and lowered the assault rifle to the floor. Wincing, she used her weapon to push up from the floor and balance herself. She walked down the hallway in Hellraiser's direction. She stole a glance at Assassin's dead body as she passed him, and spat on it. She then grabbed Hellraiser under his arm and pulled him to his feet.

"Gaaaah!" Hellraiser's face balled up in agony. He pressed his back against the wall and grabbed the handle of the bowie knife.

"Jesus." Quan cringed, seeing how far the knife was in him. He was lucky Assassin's knife game was trash. Otherwise, he would have been assed out. "I would try to pull it out for you, but my arm is busted," she told him.

"No—no—it's—it's okay," Hellraiser told her, gritting. He was pulling the knife out of him inch by inch. The color had begun to leave his face, and he was sweating something serious. "I've got—I've got—it!" He finally yanked the knife out of him, and blood squirted from the hole it had made in him. He looked at the bloody knife and dropped it to the floor. "Come on. Let's get the fuck outta here." He threw his arm around her shoulders and took the assault rifle from her. They then began walking towards the opposite end of the hallway where the stairs were located.

"Are you two all right?" Zekey asked as he stood beside Lil' Saint at the bottom of the steps. They were watching Quan help Hellraiser down the stairs.

"Quan's been shot, and I've been stabbed, but we'll live," Hellraiser said in a pained voice, holding his bleeding wound. "Listen, we don't have any time to waste. I'm sure this place has our DNA all over it, so we've gotta burn this motha down," he told them as Zekey examined Quan's wounds. He quickly tore off two ends of his shirt and tied them around her shoulder and bicep to slow her bleeding.

"I'll get the gas cans from the back of the truck," Lil' Saint said and jogged out of the mansion.

Zekey tore the end off Hellraiser's shirt and tied it around his waist to slow his bleeding. By this time, Lil' Saint had returned with two big ass red gas cans he'd taken from the Brinks truck. He kept one for himself and passed the other to Zekey, who was in the middle of kissing and rubbing on Quan.

"Quan, Zekey and I will splash this place with gasoline," Lil' Saint told her as he adjusted his eyeglasses. "You think you and Trey can manage to make it back out into the van?"

"Yeah, I've got 'em," Quan replied, wincing and getting a better hold of Hellraiser. Together, they made their way towards the double doors of the mansion. As they walked along, Hellraiser looked up and over his shoulder at a huge portrait of Hitt-Man, Assassin, and Niqua he hadn't noticed when they first stormed the mansion. He scowled and threw up his 'Fuck You' finger at it.

"Come on, Z," Lil' Saint said, tapping him and walking off to splash the mansion with gasoline. They tied bandanas around the lower half of their faces and went about the task in mind. Once they were done, they cast the empty gas cans aside, and Lil' Saint signaled for Zekey to head out the door. He pulled a Zippo lighter from out of his pocket, struck a flame, and tossed it onto the drenched carpet. *Froosh!* The fire spread throughout the mansion hastily, and he took off running out of the front door.

Lil' Saint jumped behind the wheel of the Brinks truck, fired it up, and drove away, with the raging fire of Hitt-Man's mansion illuminating the sky.

Abrafo watched from behind the wheel of his car as the Brinks truck drove down the street. He then started up his whip, busted a U-turn in the middle of the street, and drove out in the opposite direction.

***

Da Crew disposed of the Brinks truck and their assault rifles. They hopped into Lil' Saint's Cadillac and drove out to Lachaun and Hellraiser's mansion. They called for Dr. CarMichael to give them a physical examination. Zekey and Lil' Saint's injuries were minor compared to Quan and Hellraiser's wounds. Dr. CarMichael tended to their knife and gunshot wounds and gave them a prescription for a pain killa called Ultram ER. Hellraiser tried to drop a few G-stacks on him, but he refused to take them. Dr. CarMichael dapped up and hugged everyone he was familiar with and then left. Shortly, the Jameses got a call from the hospital informing them that KiMani had come out of his coma. Everyone piled in their vehicles and raced down to the hospital to see KiMani.

KiMani lay in bed watching the 25-inch flat-screen television set mounted on the wall. Interesting enough, there was a breaking news report about the fatal shootout that left several people dead, and Hitt-Man's mansion being burned down. Seeing something at the corner of his eye, KiMani looked to the doorway and saw Lachaun, Hellraiser, Lil' Saint, Billion, Zekey, and Quan entering his room.

"My baby...my baby's finally up." Lachaun's voice cracked emotionally, and tears streamed down her cheeks. She rushed over to KiMani and hugged him. He howled in pain, and she took a step back. A terrified look was on her face as she wondered what she'd done to hurt him. "KiMani, what's wrong? What did I do?"

"It's okay, Ma, you musta forgot I was shot," KiMani said, wincing and trying to adjust himself in bed to a comfortable position. He spoke in a hushed, weakened voice.

"Oh, I'm so sorry. I did." Lachaun cracked a grin. "I feel so stupid. I don't know how I forgot." She caressed his forehead, kissed him on his cheek, and rubbed his arm affectionately.

"What up, lil' man? You good?" KiMani asked Billion, who was standing with their father's arm around his shoulders.

"Yep," Billion replied. He looked like he was afraid to approach his big brother.

"Come over and say hello to your brother, Billion. Come on," Lachaun told him and motioned him over to KiMani's bedside. She then snatched some Kleenex from the small box residing on the push table and dabbed the wetness from her cheeks.

Billion walked over to KiMani's bedside. KiMani raised his hand, but Billion was scared to touch him. He feared he'd hurt him.

"What chu afraid of, lil' bro? You think you're gonna hurt me?" KiMani asked with a smirk. Billion nodded as he fidgeted with his fingers. "You're not gonna hurt me, YG. I'm sure of that. Come on, man, don't leave yo' big bro hanging."

Billion lifted his hand and did the exclusive handshake with KiMani they always did when they linked up. Billion smiled happily as his big brother rubbed his head. He pulled him closer and kissed him on his forehead. "I love yo' ol' big head ass, man," KiMani told him.

"You gotta big head," Billion fired back with a smile.

Everyone busted up laughing.

"Nigga, what?" KiMani said playfully and threw phantom punches at Billion. Billion threw some back at him. He then walked over to his big brother for a hug. KiMani hugged him and kissed him twice on his head.

Lachaun looked up at what was playing on the television. She exchanged glances with Hellraiser and nodded to the news report. He looked up at it, but then focused his attention back on KiMani. He approached his son and kissed him on his forehead and cheek.

"I love you, son. I'm glad you came back to us," Hellraiser told him.

"Glad to be back, Pops. I love you too," KiMani replied and touched fists with his old man. He looked from his father to Lil' Saint, seeing their faces were battered and bruised. "Fuck happened to y'all?"

"We took care of them bustas that got at chu and Arnez," Hellraiser told him.

"Yeah, we even made the news," Lil' Saint said to KiMani and tossed his head toward the television set. KiMani watched the TV until the report of what happened at the mansion was done.

"That's y'all old niggaz work?" KiMani asked with a smile.

"Yeah, that's our handiwork, son," Hellraiser replied with a smile and hung his arm around Lil' Saint's shoulders.

"Y'all still got it, I see," KiMani said with a smirk. When he locked eyes with Zekey, he recalled what he said to him when he was in a coma. "What's understood doesn't need to be explained. From now on, it's all love from here," he told Zekey and held his fist to his chest.

"It's all love, youngin'," Zekey replied and touched his fist to his chest. He was standing beside Quan, who had her wounded arm in a sling.

"Pops, where's Uncle Julian and Uncle Mack?" KiMani asked about the rest of his father's best friends. A saddened look came across everyone's faces, and they bowed their heads. A couple of them cleared their throats. Instantly, KiMani's eyes accumulated tears that attempted to fall from his eyes. He wiped away the dampness and sniffled, pulling on his nose. "What, uh, what happened to them?"

"To make a long story short—they all died in our honor," Hellraiser told him. "If it wasn't for your uncle Mack, no one you see here in this room would be alive right now."

Hellraiser told KiMani everything that happened since he'd been in a coma.

"I'd like for us to have a moment of silence for our brothers," Lil' Saint told everyone and then cleared his throat. "Let us all bow our heads."

Everyone bowed their heads in a moment of silence. The only sound inside the room was the medical machinery and the chit chatter between the hospital staff outside the door.

"Okay," Lil' Saint said, letting everyone know the moment of silence was over.

"Sooo, uh, KiMani, what was it like being in a coma?" Lachaun asked him as she sat on the side of his bed and caressed his head lovingly. Billion walked over to his mother and stood between her legs.

"This might sound weird, Ma, but, uh, I-I talked to God," Ki-Mani told her. His reply garnered curious stares from everyone present.

"Well, uh, honey, what did he say?" Lachaun inquired, continuously caressing his head.

"I know my calling now," KiMani answered her. "He wants me to serve him here on Earth."

***

2019
Four years later

It was 9:15 A.M., on a sunny Sunday morning, at The House of Holy Believers Church. The parking lot was packed with the vehicles of members and some visitors. There wasn't a seat available in the house. In fact, the place was so packed they had to bring out chairs so people could sit. The congregation was dressed to the nines. Their attention was focused on the prime minister as he gave his speech. A few of them wiped their sweaty foreheads and fanned themselves to keep cool.

"...Oh, yeah, I'm notta shame to admit, your minister was a sinning man," KiMani spoke into his headset's microphone as he paced the stage in his religious garb. His spiritual awakening led to him dropping his cornrows and street wear. The young brother now rocked a fade riddled with waves, nicely trimmed goatee, and designer suits. "Me and my best friend, Arnez, may he rest in peace, were terrorizing the very same neighborhood we grew up in..." He took the time to pat the sweat peppered on his forehead with his folded handkerchief. "We robbed, stole, shot folks, and sold dope...all of the things that contributed to destroying our own people and community, sadly." He cleared his throat with his fist to his mouth. "But thanks to the support of my loving family," he said, nodding to his family who were seated among the audience. They smiled proudly at their reformed son. Hellraiser hugged Lachaun and Billion around their necks affectionately. He then kissed them on the side of their heads. "And a man who I look at as an uncle, Brother Minister Markham, I sought out our Heavenly Father and HE changed my life."

Saint was sitting among his wife and kids in the pews, three rows behind the James family. He smirked at KiMani and waved at him with his Bible. KiMani adjusted his eyeglasses and gave the man a slight nod. He was about to continue with his speech until he saw Zekey and his family in the audience. A big smile spread across his face. He hadn't seen Zekey and his wife in years. They officially squashed their beef once he'd come out of his coma. "I know that isn't who I think it is out there in the audience—Zekey? Is that you, Zekey?"

KiMani jumped off the stage and made his way up the aisle. The audience turned around in their seats to see exactly who he was talking to. They laid their eyes on Zekey, who was sitting beside Quan who was holding their two-year-old son. He was asleep in her arms and drooling at the corner of his mouth.

"Yeah, it's me," Zekey said with a smile and stood to his feet. He had a shiny baldhead and a fully gray beard. He was dressed in a form-fitting, dark-burgundy suit and skinny black tie. There were gold diamond earrings in his lobes and a Cuban-link bracelet around his wrist.

"I haven't seen you in years, brotha. Gemme a hug, man." KiMani smiled harder and opened his arms wide. Zekey also smiled harder and embraced him, patting him on his back. KiMani held him at arm's length and took a good look at him. He'd packed on a few pounds since he'd stopped putting that shit up his nose, but he looked damn good. "It's good to see you, black man. It's really good to see you."

"It's good to see you too," Zekey replied, nodding and chewing his gum.

"Gemme another hug, brotha," KiMani told him, and they hugged again. He then looked around at his audience with his hand on Zekey's shoulder. "My beloved Brothas and Sistas, believe it or not, this is an enemy turned friend of mine. Back in the day, this brotha and I used to be at each other's throats, tryna kill each other..." KiMani went on to tell the audience about how the drama between him and Zekey started. Of course, he left out the murders. He wasn't a fool. There wasn't any statute of limitations on that shit. He then told them how they'd put the past behind them and moved forward with their lives. "What are you doing witcho self now, brotha?"

"My beautiful wife and I wear many hats, young bruh," Zekey told him humbly. "But my bread and butter are real estate and…" Zekey went on to tell the audience how he and Quan were making their living. In the middle of giving his explanation, he introduced everyone to Quan and their son. Everyone was so caught up in the moment they were ignorant of the stranger that had entered the House of Worship. He was wearing black sunglasses, a hood over his head, and a duster. The high temperatures of the outside and his being warmly dressed had him sweating. He could feel the beads of sweat sliding down the sides of his face, but he ignored them. The mission at hand was his only concern, and no one was going to stop him from doing what he came there to do.

Abrafo, the stranger, casually walked down the aisle with one hand at his side and the other tucked in the pocket of his duster. On the inside of his duster, he was toting something big, long, and deadly. The further he advanced down the aisle, the more eyes of the audience he drew. They looked at him strangely as he passed them, wondering what was going on. The presence of Abrafo drew the attention of Hellraiser. He shot out of his seat and instinctively went to draw his gun. His hand came up empty, and he realized he no longer packed a blower because he wasn't about that life anymore.

"KiMani, look out!" Hellraiser called out to his son and took off in his direction, knocking people out of the way. He moved as fast as he could, jumping from the back rests of pews, trying to make it to his boy before it was too late. Everything seemed to be moving in slow motion at this point, as more and more people were taking notice. Zekey spotted Abrafo and rushed to cover his wife and kid. When KiMani saw him, his eyes widened and his mouth hung open. He was frozen in place and couldn't seem to move.

At this time, Lil' Saint saw the danger KiMani was in and knew he had to act fast. He told his wife and kids to get down and then opened his Bible. A .45 semi-automatic pistol was wedged inside of an opening he'd cut into the scriptures. Swiftly, he pulled out his piece and tossed the holy book aside. Determination was written across his face as he made his way towards Abrafo. He extended his gun to take a shot at him, but frightened people got in his way. They were ducking and running across his line of vision.

Abrafo threw open his duster and upped his shotgun. He leveled it at KiMani's chest and pulled the trigger. The shotgun jerked and flames erupted out of its barrel. KiMani's face balled up and he clenched his teeth, taking the blast full-on in the chest. The impact spun him around in a 180-degree turn. Abrafo pumped his shotgun again, leveled it, and pulled the trigger again. *Bloom!* The second blast propelled KiMani forward, and he fell on the side of his face. His eyes were wide and vacant while his mouth was ajar. He was dead as a mothafucka!

"Noooo!" Lachaun hollered out, seeing her stepson get his back blown out. She was shielding Billion with tears in her eyes. As bad as she wanted to go after him, she couldn't. She had to protect her last living son.

"Mothafuckaaaa!" Hellraiser shrilled at Abrafo as he leaped off the pews and tackled him. They crashed to the floor and slid in between the pews on the other side of the church. Abrafo lost his shotgun somewhere far underneath another row of pews. "I'll kill you, I'll fucking kill you!" a teary-eyed Hellraiser spat in a rage and threw his fists down into Abrafo's face, one after the other. The vicious blow broke his sunglasses, busted his nose, and bloodied his grill. Abrafo grabbed him by either of his wrists and slammed his forehead into his nose and mouth. The impact broke his nose and bloodied his mouth. He dripped blood all over his white button-down and suit. He was then kneed in his jewels and booted in the chest. He flew backwards and slid out into the aisle.

Abrafo turned on his side, spitting blood on the floor. He jabbed a loose tooth in his mouth, then pulled it out and looked at it. He threw the bloody tooth aside and got up from the floor. He whipped back around and pulled two guns from his shoulder holsters. By this time, the church was halfway full on account of

151

most of the audience having cleared out through the front door. Still, there were some of them running back and forth down the aisle, tripping and falling over KiMani's dead body. Abrafo could see Lil' Saint trying desperately to draw a bead on him, but innocent people were in his way. Unfortunately for those innocent people, Abrafo didn't give a fuck about them, which was why he started busting at them to clear a path.

Boc, boc, boc, boc, boc!

Several people fell to their deaths, and even more hit the floor seriously wounded. The fleeing people screamed louder than they had before and ran a tad faster. They bumped into each other and fell. Then scrambled back up on their feet and kept running. Now Abrafo's path to Lil' Saint was visible, and vice versa. They drew down on each other, but one was just a bit faster than the other.

Boc, boc, boc, boc!

"Aaaah!" Lil' Saint hollered out as he was struck. He dropped his gun and turned around, bumping into the back of the pews on the side of him. He was bleeding badly from his chest and mouth. He looked to where he'd told his wife and children to take cover. He found them looking at him with ugly faces and snotty noses, crying. His vision was blurry and came in and out of focus. He took a step forward, but his legs buckled under him, and he dropped down to one knee. He went to get up again, but Abrafo came up behind him. He pressed one of his guns at the top of his head and pulled its trigger. Bloody brain fragments and pieces of skull flew upward like a geyser. Lil' Saint's eyes rolled into the back of his head, and he fell to the floor. His family screamed hysterically and cried seeing him get downed by the big African.

After Abrafo assassinated Lil' Saint, he set his sights on Hellraiser. He found him in great pain, crawling toward the shotgun he'd lost when he'd tackled him. Abrafo pressed his boot against the center of his back, popped two into the back of his head, and made his way down the aisle. He saw Lachaun running towards the back of the church with Billion in her arms, but he wasn't the least concerned with them. He had to make sure the main nigga he'd come for was gone for good.

The church was nearly empty by the time Abrafo made it over to KiMani. He emptied his guns into the young man's lifeless form, making his thick blood ooze out beneath him. The last of the congregation had left the church when he started reloading his bangaz.

Blowl, blowl, blowl!

Two bullets missed Abrafo, but one of them slammed into his back and made him stumble. He looked to his side and saw Zekey coming at him, letting his gun talk. The big African whipped around, tucking one of his guns and running for the entrance of the church. As he fled, he reloaded his remaining gun to keep Zekey off his ass and find an escape route.

"Don't run now, nigga! It's killa versus killa!" Zekey roared, sending fire at Abrafo's back as he chased him up the aisle. "Killa versus killa!"

When Zekey started busting at Abrafo, Quan, with their baby boy, escaped through the back door of the holy tenement. It was all a part of Zekey's plan: keep the assassin distracted while his family fled to safety.

As soon as Abrafo spilled out of the church, he was struck by a black Lincoln Town Car with pitch-black tinted windows. He flipped over the hood of the car and crashed to the pavement, losing his gun in the process. Zekey smiled devilishly, figuring he had the shooter at his mercy. At the same time, he ran up on the Lincoln's hood to finish off Abrafo, Tulip, wearing a ski mask over her face and black sunglasses over her eyes, appeared out of nowhere. She upped her gun as Zekey went to shoot Abrafo and sent three shots at him. Zekey howled in agony as he was struck in his side. He dropped his banga, fell backward off the Lincoln, and hit the pavement on his stomach.

The doors of the Lincoln Town Car popped open, and two Mexican men hopped out. The sun gleamed off their bald heads as they came from either side of the Town Car. One grabbed Zekey underneath his arms and drug him towards their whip while the other played lookout with an Uzi. While this was taking place, Tulip was helping Abrafo to his feet so they could flee the area.

Once she'd gotten him up on his booted feet, they ran as far as they could to their getaway car.

"Vamos tonto, vamos, vamos, vamos (Come on, fool, let's go, let's go, let's go)!" the Mexican that had stored Zekey into the back of the Lincoln shouted as he hung halfway out of the window and waved his comrade on. The Mexican man holding the Uzi slowly backed up towards the Lincoln, looking around for anyone that posed a threat. When he didn't see any, he hopped back into the Lincoln, slammed the door shut, and shouted to the driver to drive off in Spanish.

Quan deposited her baby boy inside of his car seat, grabbed a gun from underneath the passenger seat, and then cocked its slide. Tears spilled down her cheeks as she fled the car and left its passenger door open. She ran as fast as she could across the parking lot towards the car the Mexicans had stashed her husband in.

"Noooo, noooo, nooooo!" Quan shouted over and over again, with tears flooding her cheeks. She saw the Lincoln Town Car pulling off and knew she'd never see her man again if it got away. She slowed to a stop, parted her legs, and upped her gun, with both hands. As the Lincoln drove away, she sent shot after shot at them.

Blam, blam, blam, blam, blam!

Quan's gun resonated loudly and dangerously with fire erupting out of its barrel. Every shot she sent at the Lincoln Town Car deflected off its body with a spark. Her gun's bullets proved to be harmless and only left scratches behind. The vehicle was not only bulletproof but it was also bomb proof. Still, that didn't stop Quan from chasing after it and continuously firing at it.

Blam, blam, blam, blam, blam!

More sparks flew off the Lincoln as it was met with more firepower from Quan's gun. Realizing her efforts of saving her husband were futile, she broke down sobbing with a snotty nose. Bowing her head, she wiped her eyes and sniffled aloud. Hearing running feet at her right, Quan turned around to see Abrafo and Tulip running towards their getaway car. Back-to-back imagery assaulted her mind of the big African gunning down several people. She saw the entire tragedy being his fault. The chaos he caused led to the event of her husband being stolen from her and her children's lives.

Quan ran over to Abrafo and Tulip's getaway car. They'd just slammed the doors and Abrafo had just fired the vehicle up. Quan parted her legs again and upped her banga. Abrafo froze when he saw the crying, snot-nosed woman with her bead on him. He knew she had him dead to rights. Now he was just waiting for the hot ones that would end his existence.

Quan mad dogged Abrafo and tightened her jaws. She then pulled the trigger of her gun with extreme hatred. *Click, click, click!* Her brows furrowed when her gun didn't fire. She looked at her piece like it was a foreign object, realizing she'd used all her bullets on the Lincoln Town Car. When she looked back up at Abrafo, he was coming at her full speed ahead with intentions of mowing her ass down. At the last minute, she was able to dive out of the way and miss the car by a foot.

Skirrrrrt!

The getaway car squealed as it peeled out of the parking lot, leaving smoke clouds behind.

Quan sat up on her side on the ground, looking at the vehicle get away. She cried in silence with trembling shoulders, big teardrops falling from her eyes and splashing on the pavement. Her entire world had just exploded into a million pieces, and there wasn't any way she could put it back together.

"Noooo, noooo, noooooo!" Quan screamed over and over again, tears bursting from her eyes as she pounded the asphalt with her fist.

A police helicopter flew over the area and police car sirens consumed the air. The two sounds meshed together with the sobs of Quan's broken heart and pained soul.

"Whyyyyy? Oh, God, oh, God! Whyyyyy?"

Tranay Adams

Chapter Twelve

It was one in the afternoon as a pearl-white Escalade truck coasted up the road past farms on either side of it. The Mexicans figured the police would be looking for the vehicle they used in Zekey's kidnapping, so they set it ablaze and picked up the SUV. Zekey sat in the middle of the two Mexican niggaz that had snatched him up. He was sweaty and wincing from being shot. He took his hand from his wounds, and it was masked with blood. He leaned his head back against the seat and shut his eyes, swallowing his spit. He listened to the Mexicans as they talked in Spanish, laughed at God only knew what, and passed a joint around. Zekey didn't have the slightest idea of what Changa's goons had in store for him, but he was sure the levels of torture he'd experience would be legendary. With all the dirt he'd done in the streets, whatever punishment awaited him, he was sure he was deserving of it.

"Fuck it. It is what it is," Zekey said under his breath.

"Unc! Aye, Unc!" a voice called out to Zekey.

Zekey's forehead creased, and his eyes popped open. He looked around to find the Mexicans still talking among each other in Spanish, but he didn't know which of them called for him.

"I'm right here, nigga." The voice spoke from his right.

Zekey looked to his right at the passenger window and found a hologram image of Arnez sitting next to the door on the opposite side. When he looked to the other side of the car, there wasn't anyone there, so he focused his attention back on the first window. Arnez was there smiling at him. He managed to smile back at him.

"Blood, I haven't seen you in a hot minute," Zekey told him weakly. "Where you been, man? I missed yo' ass, I missed yo' ass a lot." He swore, his voice cracked emotionally and his eyes became teary.

"I missed you too. But it's all good, we'll be together sooner than you think," Arnez assured him. "As far as where I've been? I've always been witchu—right here." He pointed to his temple. "And right here." He placed his hand over the left side of his chest. "I never left you, Unc. Never."

Zekey nodded understandingly as tears slid down his cheeks. One of the Mexicans noticed the tears sliding down his face and called for the others' attention to look at him. They all glanced at him.

"Big bad, tough guy is crying like a little bitch," the Mexican sitting to the left of Zekey said.

"He's gonna be doing a hell of a lot more than crying once Changa and Larenz get a hold of 'em," the Mexican behind the wheel assured him, glancing up at Zekey through the rearview mirror.

"You know, believe it or not, I feel sorry for this son of a bitch," the Mexican riding shotgun up front said. "Jefe and his cousin are gonna get medieval on this mayate."

Smack!

The Mexican sitting to the right of Zekey brought his opened hand across his face viciously, leaving a red hand impression behind. Zekey winced, feeling the stinging sensation on his cheek, but he was entirely too weak to put up a fight.

"Ah, I don't feel sorry for this black piece of shit," he claimed, frowning. "You fuck with the toro and you get the horns."

"Nosotros estamos aqui (We're here)," the Mexican behind the wheel announced as they pulled up to the doors of a barn.

Two Mexicans in all black with the straps of their M-16s slung over their shoulders opened the enormous doors of the barn. Once the Escalade truck drove inside, they closed the doors back and placed the latches across it. The Mexicans sitting on either side of Zekey hopped out of the SUV, grabbed him under his arms, and drug him towards the center of the barn. Zekey's head bobbled and he dripped blood on the hay below him. The loss of blood had left him lightheaded and exhausted. He could hear the horses in the nearby stables making noises as he was pulled forward. The overwhelming smell of the horses, manure, feed, silage, and wood filling his nostrils threatened to gag him. The odor was something he could never see himself getting used to.

The Mexicans, breathing heavily, stopped Zekey at Changa and Larenz's feet. The two men were shirtless and had big ass machetes sheathed at their sides. Though Changa was an old man, he had a big, muscular, tattooed body, and so did Larenz. They both had some very interesting ink, but the ones they had in common stood out the most. They were those of Travieso and Maria's faces on their chests with roses below them and Rest in Paradise Familia. Maria was the little girl that Zekey shot in the head the night he and KiMani went after Travieso.

"I haven't killed anyone in twenty-five years, negrito, but today I come outta retirement," Changa told Zekey as he held him by his lower jaw and looked into his eyes. He then harped up mucus and spat in his face twice. The nasty goo slid down his face and hung off his chin like small ropes.

"Remember me, bitch?" Larenz said, stepping forth smiling wickedly. He was a narrow-face dude who sported a fade and a goatee. He stood five-foot-eight and weighed every bit of 175 lbs. A colostomy bag hung from his left side and it had liquid feces in it. "It's 'cause of you I'll have to wear this shit bag for the rest of my life, hijo de puta!" He punched Zekey in the jaw and sent blood flying. Zekey's head dropped and his bleeding mouth pelted the ground below. Larenz was the one he'd shot in the ribs during the dice game that he and his boyz tried to cheat him in.

Changa drew his machete from his sheath and held it at his side. "Strip 'em!" he commanded loud and clear. Larenz drew his machete and came to stand beside his uncle. He sharpened his machete on a sharpening block then passed the block to his uncle, who did the same. Together, they watched as the Mexicans that brought Zekey to the barn stripped him naked and dragged him before them.

Larenz licked his thumb and pressed it against his machete. A trickle of blood ran down his thumb and he sucked it off. He and his uncle got on either side of Zekey as he lay bleeding on the hay-covered ground. His eyes were hooded and he was pale. On top of that, his breathing was shallow.

"Come on, Unc, let's go home." Arnez appeared and extended his hand down to Zekey.

159

"Home—yeah—I wanna go home," Zekey replied in a whisper and grabbed hold of Arnez's hand. As soon as the young man pulled him upward, Changa swung his machete downward with a grunt. The machete sunk halfway into Zekey's skull, and blood speckled Changa's face and body. Zekey was already dead, so he didn't feel a thing. He'd left the vessel he occupied while on Earth to go to a paradise with his nephew.

"Ugh!" Larenz grunted as he swung his machete into Zekey's hip, speckling his face with blood. He wiped his face with the back of his hand and unintentionally smeared the blood across it. He then gritted and swung the machete again and again and again. He and Changa worked together, butchering Zekey's lifeless form. More and more blood speckled their faces and bodies. They laughed and smiled wickedly as they attacked him savagely. The rest of the Mexicans stood by, watching the animalistic behavior of their boss and his relative.

Arnez and Zekey, with their arms around each other's shoulders, walked towards the doors of the barn. The doors opened and a blinding white light shone inside.

"Aye, what's it like up there?" Zekey asked.

"You mean down there?" Arnez replied. Zekey looked at him fearfully. "Hahahaha! Chill, Unc, I'm just fucking witchu," he assured him. "I don't wanna spoil it for you. But believe me, you're gonna love it. That's my word."

Arnez and Zekey disappeared into the light while Changa and Larenz continued to hack away at Zekey's bloody, mutilated body.

***

That night

Abrafo's face was on every news channel as the primary suspect in what the media was calling The House of Holy Believers Church Massacre. His face and name were also plastered on every social media platform there was, and radio stations were even talking about what had gone down. Abrafo was as hot as an

African summer in the streets, which was why he'd planned to get his family, collect his bag for the hit, and get his ass back home to Ghana. He already brokered a deal with a coyote who guaranteed his safe passage back to the Motherland. Now, all he had to do was get his bread from Assassin's attorney, Rick Gold, grab his oldest son, Dexter, from Tulip's best friend's house, and link up with the coyote.

"Baby, did you tell Joy to get Dexter ready so we can pick him up?" Abrafo asked as he backed into a parking space and turned off his whip.

Tulip looked up from her cellphone. "I called her five times and I left her messages, but she hasn't called me back yet. I even texted her."

"Knowing Joy, she's probably passed out drunk. We'll just head on over once we leave here," Abrafo told her. She nodded with a worried look on her face. Using his curled finger, he tilted her chin up so she'd be looking into his eyes. "Hey, everything is going to be okay. Trust me, my beautiful Tulip." He lovingly kissed her lips, her cheeks, and then her forehead. "Tell Mommy, princess, tell her everything is going to be okay and to trust Daddy." He smiled as he rubbed Tulip's big round belly.

Tulip smiled down at her belly, holding it with both hands. Abrafo kissed her belly and opened the door to get out the car. He was about to step out when Tulip grasped his shoulder. He turned around to her, and she cupped his face, tonguing him down. She pecked him on the lips one last time, and he hopped out. She watched him closely as he slammed the door behind him and made his way around the front of their whip. Tulip was smiling hard, showcasing her pearly white teeth. She appeared to be glowing in that moment. She was head over heels in love with him, and her head was far in the clouds.

Tulip honked the horn and drew his attention. When he stopped and looked in her direction, she hung halfway out of the window and yelled out, "I love you," blowing a kiss and then waving at him. He smiled and yelled that he "loved her, too," before proceeding to the suite Assassin's attorney worked out of.

He stared down at the attorney's business card as he walked up the stairs, gliding his hand up the guardrail. He reached the second level, looking at the suite number on every door he passed. Something told him to look down at the parking lot and when he did, he saw Tulip smiling and waving at him. He returned the gesture and continued his search for the suite. As soon as he found it, he opened the door and walked in. The place was made up like the waiting room inside a dentist's office with rows of chairs, used magazines on small tables, a water dispenser with a stack of small Styrofoam cups on the side of it, and a 32-inch flat screen mounted on the wall.

The waiting room was completely empty, but there was a well-dressed receptionist at the window. She was a chocolate sister with her hair pulled back in a bun. She wore a white blouse with ruffling around its collar and wrists. Her head was tilted to the side, and her shoulder was holding the telephone to her ear. She was too busy running her mouth on the jack and filing down her fingernails to notice Abrafo's presence. He stood there waiting for her to acknowledge him so he could holla at the attorney and get his payment.

"Biiiiitch, I know you're lying! Unh unh, shut up!" the receptionist said into the telephone. Abrafo cleared his throat, but the bitch was still bumping her gums like he wasn't there. Since that didn't get her attention, he cleared his throat louder, with his fist to his mouth. Instantly, she stopped filing her nails and rolled her eyes at him. "Girl, lemme call you back. Someone just walked in," she told whomever on the telephone. "Alright." She disconnected the cordless telephone and placed it back on the desk top. "How may I help you?" she asked Abrafo with her eyes on her nails, steadily filing them. She stopped for a moment to take a good look at them before going right back to business.

"I'm here to see Attorney Rick Gold," Abrafo informed her.

"Do you have an appointment?" she asked.

"No. He told me to just drop by, and he'd inform whomever at the front desk that I was coming."

"Ooooh, okay, now I know who you are," she told him. "You're the African guy. You can go right in after you hear the buzzer."

"Thank you."

"Ummmm hmmm," she said, and began working on the nails on her other hand.

"Say, uh, do we know each other from somewhere? You look real familiar."

She took him in from head to toe then looked him directly in his eyes. "Nah, sweetie, I'm sure I don't know you. You're not my type."

Abrafo nodded and walked toward the door. A buzzer went off, signaling for him to enter through the door, so he pulled it open and walked inside. He could hear the receptionist shouting to him the directions to Attorney Gold's office. Once he'd finally reached the attorney's office door, he knocked on it and was extended an invitation inside.

When Abrafo entered through the door, he saw the big executive office chair that Gold normally sat in with its back to him. Usually Gold would be goofing around in his office while talking on his Bluetooth and bouncing a tennis ball off the wall. Gold was a real jovial cat that joked around. He loved sports cars, skinny, young white women with huge breasts, white Russians, and partying on his yacht. An icy chill slid down the middle of Abrafo's back as he stood in the middle of the office. He couldn't shake the creepy feeling that overcame him. He didn't know exactly what was wrong, but something definitely wasn't right.

"Mr. Gold, I'd like to get my payment so I can get outta here," Abrafo told him in his thick accent. "I don't know if you've noticed, but my face is plastered on nearly every news channel in the country. I have to get outta the United States—how you Americans say? ASAP."

"My nigga, you're not getting jack shit," Gold replied from the executive chair.

Abrafo frowned, and his top lip peeled back in a sneer. He balled his fists, and the veins in them became pronounced. "What?"

"You heard me you big, black, dumb, spear-chucking fuck!"

"I'll fuckin' kill you, you son of a beech!" Abrafo growled angrily and charged towards Gold's desk. Right then, the office doors swung open and two masked men ran inside. They were dressed in all black from head to toe and holding Escrima sticks that doubled as tasers.

Abrafo, hearing the masked men enter the office, turned around to them. He threw a haymaker at the one on his right, but he ducked him and zapped Abrafo in the back of his kneecap.

"Aaaaaah!" Abrafo threw his head back, screaming, and dropped down to one knee. "Rraaaah!" he screamed even louder when the other masked man zapped him in the neck with his stick. The one that had zapped him in the back of his kneecap kicked him in his jaw, and his blood dotted up the wall. Abrafo fell on his side and attempted to get up again, but he was kicked in his mouth. He fell back to the floor, bleeding at the mouth with two broken front teeth. He lay there as the masked men kicked, stomped, and assaulted him with their Escrima sticks. They didn't stop until their arms were tired and they were breathing hard. They were sweating so profusely behind their masks they pulled them off and held them at their sides. The men behind the masks weren't men at all. They were women: Lachaun and Quan to be exact.

"Bitch-ass nigga!" Lachaun scowled and spat a loogey on his face. Quan spat a loogey on his face too. Then, to add insult to injury, the bitch kicked him in his stomach. He grimaced and groaned in pain, holding himself.

The big executive chair slowly spun around to reveal Dr. CarMichael sitting in it. He was wearing a navy-blue turtleneck and black slacks. Abrafo's five-year-old son, Dexter, was sitting in his lap. The boy's eyeglasses were crooked on his face as he uselessly struggled to get away. The doctor had one latex-gloved hand over the child's mouth while the other gloved hand held the syringe of the needle in the vein in his neck. Dr. CarMichael, who wore a solemn expression on his face, held fast to Dexter as he tried his best to break free of him. While this was happening, the doctor started talking to Abrafo.

"You know those people you killed? Well, they were good friends of mine," Dr. CarMichael informed him. "Treymaine and Saint bought me my first car, paid for me to go to medical school, and all of my expenses while attending. They even took care of my family while I was away. And KiMani, that twenty-four-year-old, God-fearing young man you murdered in cold blood, he was my god-son," he told him, with tears running unevenly down his cheeks. Dexter was still struggling to break his hold, but he didn't seem to mind. The boy was proving to be an annoyance, but it wasn't anything he couldn't handle.

"You hurt 'em—you hurt 'em and I'll snap your spine in—Aah!" Abrafo hollered as Quan whacked him across the back of his head with her Escrima stick. He fell face down in the carpet, grimacing from the painful blow.

"You're in no position to threaten me, homeboy!" Dr. CarMichael told him. "As a matter of fact, you should be groveling at my fucking feet, begging me to spare your life and those of your family!"

"Lemme go! Lemme go, goddamn it!" Tulip's screaming could be heard as she struggled to break free from whomever was dragging her down the hallway.

"Tulip? Tulip?" Abrafo called out to his wife between grimacing and pushing up from the floor.

"I swear to God, if you don't let me go, I'll—" Tulip was cut short by a vicious smack to her face. The three pounds of pressure behind the blow left her moaning and barely conscious. When Abrafo looked to the door, a saggy-cheek, seventy-five-year-old black man with black moles on his face neared the office. He wore an Apple Jack hat and overcoat. His wrinkled, vein-riddled hand was gripping a walking cane and leading the way. Abrafo saw great sadness in the older man's eyes. He'd never laid eyes on him before, so he didn't have the slightest idea of what heartache he'd caused him.

Once the old man had stepped inside of the office, two Italian men drug Tulip inside behind him. Her head was bowed and her knees were being dragged across the carpeted floor.

"Tulip! Tulip!" Abrafo called her name over and over again as he reached out to her. His eyes slowly pooled with tears and threatened to spill down his cheeks. Though he was a killa with a heart the temperature of an iceberg, his children and his wife were his Kryptonite. In other words, they were his weakness!

"Uhhh! Abra—Abrafo?" Tulip asked, bringing up her bobbling head, wincing. The side of her face was red and swollen from being smacked inside the corridor.

"Yes, it's me! It's me, baby!" Abrafo cried out. "I love you. I love you so much."

"I—I love you, too, baby," Tulip cried out as well, tears sliding down her cheeks.

Right then, the clerk at the front desk, Drascilla, stepped inside the office and locked the door behind her. A hostile expression was on her face as she pulled the pins out of her bun and shook her hair loose. Her long, silky hair fell over her shoulder and down her back. The strands hanging over her face partially hid it in the shadows, but her unforgiving eyes were visible. When she came inside the office, the tension seemed to thicken, and those at her mercy were worried about what was to come.

"Aaah, fuck! You lil' shit!" Dr. CarMichael hollered out and looked to his palm where he'd been bitten. The glove was torn and had the imprint of bloody teeth marks.

"Mommy, Daddy, help me, please!" Dexter called out to his parents. He attempted to hop off Dr. CarMichael's lap, but he snatched him back fast, making his eyeglasses fall to the floor. He held the boy against him with his hand pressed down hard over his mouth. He slipped the needle of the syringe back inside the vein in his neck.

"Stopppp! What are you doing to our son?" Tulip hollered at him. Her face was soaked with tears and snot was oozing out of her nose and over her top lip.

"Please, I beg of you, don't hurt 'em! Whatever you plan to do to my child, do to me!" Abrafo pleaded for his oldest son's life. The tears he'd shed had begun drying on his cheeks.

"Oh, you most definitely gonna get yours," Dr. CarMichael assured him. "In fact, every last one of you will, and that's a promise."

Abrafo punched Quan in the gut, doubling her over. He then swept Lachaun's legs from under her, and she hit the floor, bumping her head. Snarling, he got halfway up on his feet to pounce on Dr. CarMichael, but the old man pulled out a gun with a silencer on it the size of a Pepsi can. He fired two precise shots at the back of the big African's kneecaps. He hollered out in excruciation and fell to the carpeted floor, bleeding everywhere.

Quan got up to her feet and pulled Lachaun up to hers. Wincing, she thanked her and rubbed the back of her head.

"Ugh, ooooh, my knees, my knees!" Abrafo complained and grimaced as he turned over on his back. He sat up and looked at his kneecaps. While one was oozing blood, the other one was spurting it, and then it just leaked. Abrafo moaned and groaned as he used his elbows to scoot back against the wall, dragging his legs across the carpet. Once he reached the wall, he laid his head back against it and rested his arms at his sides. At the corner of his eyes, he watched Dr. CarMichael with his son. He was powerless to stop him, so all he could do was hope he didn't kill him.

"By the way you're looking at me, I know you're wondering what this shit is in this syringe," Dr. CarMichael told him. He was looking as serious as HIV-positive test results. Dexter was still trying to get away from him, but he had a hold like a King Cobra. "Well, they call this El veneno del Diablo, which means The Devil's Venom. It's a deadly pentobarbital used to euthanize pets. It's illegal here in America, but in Mexico it's just 30 bucks a dose," he told him. "But if enough of it is given to humans, it can give them a painless death within a minute or two." He smiled evilly and looked at Dexter, who was still fighting to get away.

"Oh, no, please! I beg of you, don't!" Tulip begged, sobbing uncontrollably. "Have mercy!"

"No, please, don't! I'll do whatever you want! I swear it!" Abrafo cried and pleaded with his fingers interlocked.

"This can't be the big, bad-ass African I heard about in the streets," Dr. CarMichael said, shaking his head in disappointment. "My, my, my, it's amazing how a man can be reduced to a whiny lil' bitch when the lives of his loved ones are on the line," he told him. "Well, now you get to feel the torment and pain my friends' family and I felt when you took them away." With that, he pushed down on the feeder, and the illegal liquid substance entered Dexter's bloodstream. The drug began to take effect, slowing the child's movements and causing his eyes to flutter. The boy's parents looked on, sobbing and hollering while Dr. CarMichael stared down at him. "Look, the venom's already at work," he said, stroking Dexter's forehead like a loving mother. "It's reducing the activity of nerves, causing his muscles to relax. Then it reduces his heart rate, breathing, and blood pressure." Thirty seconds later, Dexter's eyes closed, his heart stopped, and he went limp in Dr. CarMichael's arms. He took a gander at his timepiece then looked up at the boy's parents. "That's it. He's gone to a better place now."

When Dr. CarMichael said this, Tulip and Abrafo broke down sobbing hard and loud. The doctor smacked everything off the desk top, laid Dexter down on it, and then draped his suit's jacket over him. He then walked around the desk and sat on the corner of it. He crossed his legs and rested his interlocked hands on his knee.

"You shouldn't take it so hard," Dr. CarMichael told Tulip and Abrafo. "Your son had a quick and painless death, honestly. I pushed for that to happen," he assured them. "The Markhams"— he motioned to the old man and the young lady standing beside him—"they wanted the boy to suffer like Saint and his family suffered when you murdered him."

The old man, who was Patrick Markham, Lil' Saint's father, passed the gun with the silencer on it to Drascilla and stepped forward. He took hold of his cane by its handle and shaft. His eyes were glassy and filled with hurt. Tears slowly seeped from his eyes. Losing his wife to a brain aneurism thirty years ago was devastating, but losing his only son sent his entire world crashing down.

Besides Tulip's sniffling and whimpering, the office was quiet. Abrafo was silently crying, and blood was continuing to ooze out of his kneecaps. He felt weaker than he'd ever been. His wife at the mercy of his enemy's gun and his son executed in front of him left him mentally and physically exhausted. He didn't know how much more he could take before he died from a broken heart.

Tranay Adams

Chapter Thirteen

"Young man, you took my boy away from me," Patrick began. "I would most definitely wish the heartache I experienced on my worst enemy." A teardrop fell from his eye, and he wiped away the wetness it left behind before putting his hand back on the cane. "In fact, I'd make sure he got it—tenfold!" His face balled up with hatred and made him look demonic. Gritting, he pressed a button on top of his cane, and a seven-inch blade sprang forward. *Sniiiikt!* It twinkled at its tip.

"Noooooo!" Abrafo's eyes exploded open seeing old man Patrick's intentions. Using his arms, he desperately tried to reach Tulip before any harm could come to her, but he'd never succeed in rescuing her. Lachaun and Quan zapped him in his neck and back with their Escrima sticks. And then, they kicked him in his head and ribs. He gritted in pain and still tried to get to Tulip, so they beat his ass harder. Eventually, he collapsed back to the floor, and they beat him until there wasn't any more fight in him.

"Hold his face up, I want 'em to see this!" Patrick shouted with spit flying from his lips. He snatched off his Apple Jack hat and tossed it aside. Once Lachaun and Quan were holding Abrafo up under his arms and forcing him to watch, Patrick proceeded with what he had in mind to do to Tulip. Holding the cane-like spear with both hands, he grunted and slammed its blade into her pregnant belly seven times and twisted it inside of her on the seventh. When Patrick yanked the blade out of her, blood came along with it, splattering on the floor. Her stomach spurted blood until it eventually started dripping.

"Nooooo! Oh, God, oh, God, oh, God!" Tulip screamed and cried, veins bulging on her forehead and neck. There was snot sliding out of her nostrils and small ropes of slimy spit hanging from her bottom lip. Abrafo was screaming just as loud as she was, with a runny nose and spit clinging to his lips. His head bowed and his body rocked as he sobbed. His teardrops fell rapidly, hitting the floor below.

"You see that, huh? Huh? You see that?" Patrick roared, more spit flying from his lips. "Ain't so fun when the rabbit's got the gun, now is it? I ain't done witchu yet, you big African son of a bitch," he assured Abrafo as tears slid down his cheeks. "Hold his head up! Hold it all the way up so his ass can see this!" Lachaun and Quan did like they were ordered. Abrafo and Tulip locked eyes and exchanged 'I love yous.' They knew what was coming, and there wasn't anything they could do to stop it. Patrick did a 180-degree turn, swinging his cane-like spear around.

Sniiiikt!

The bloody seven-inch blade swiped across Tulip's jugular, and instantly, blackish-red blood spilled down her chest in a river. Her eyes doubled in size, and she threw her head back. She gagged and gasped for air to no avail. The Italian men released her, and she plopped to the floor like a fish out of water. She held her neck, gasping and crawling towards Abrafo. Patrick pressed the button on the handle of his cane, and the blade retracted back into the end of it. He nodded to Lachaun and Quan, and they released a tormented Abrafo. He and Tulip crawled towards each other as fast as they could. Tulip had lost so much blood, she was weak and light headed. She stopped crawling and reached her bloody hand out to Abrafo. Her neck spurted blood out on the carpeted floor as she waited for him to reach her. He interlocked his fingers with her bloody ones. Looking her in her eyes, he told her how much she meant to him and how much he loved her.

"I—I—I love—love you—you—too—" Tulip said her last words and then took her last breath. Her head dropped to the floor, and her fingers became still. Abrafo wept, bowed his forehead to her hand, and then kissed it affectionately.

Abrafo's attention was then stolen from the ringing and vibration of his cellular. He looked down at his pocket and then up at Dr. CarMichael. He gave him a nod and told him to go ahead and answer it. Abrafo frowned, thinking it was odd that the doctor was going to allow him to answer his cell phone, but his curiosity got the best of him. He pulled his cell out of his pocket and looked at its display. Rick Gold was Facetiming him! He accepted the call.

A brown-eyed white man with a clean-shaven face appeared. His blonde hair was parted on the side and combed to the left to hide his bald spot. He wore eyeglasses with rectangle-shaped lenses and a gold necklace with a Star of David charm. The dome light was on in his car while he was driving. He occasionally glanced at his cellphone, which was attached to the holder on the dashboard.

"Hey there, buddy, I can only imagine how you're feeling right now," Rick Gold told him. "This whole situation is fucked up. I just want chu to know this is business, it's not personal."

"It's not personal? It's 'cause of you my entire family is dead," Abrafo said through clenched jaws.

"I know, buddy, and I'm sorry. I truly am," Rick Gold assured him. "But, Jesus Christ on the cross, not only did I get to keep the other half of your payment, but the good doctor there threw inna bag that looked like a fucking social security number," he told him. "I know I'm playing up the whole greedy Jew stereotype, but once I saw all that cash in those two briefcases, there was no fucking way I was turning it—"

Ka-Boom!

Rick Gold's car abruptly exploded, and Abrafo laughed heartily. The Facetime call ended, and he tossed his cellular aside. At least now that he knew he was going to die, the bastard that betrayed him was going along for the ride as well.

"I bet chu he wishes he would have thoroughly checked those briefcases now that his thirsty ass is somewhere in Jew Heaven," Dr. CarMichael said as he dangled the detonator between his legs. "That way, he would have found that bomb in between the stacks of that fugazi ass money I gave 'em."

"Well, I hate to be the one to be rude, but the night's not getting any younger," Drascilla said as she walked up to Abrafo with the blower Patrick had given her.

Abrafo yanked the amulet necklace from around his neck and looked at it. It was supposed to bring its wearer good luck and protection. But given his current situation, he knew that was a crock of shit. "Humph." He threw the amulet necklace aside, held Tulip's hand with both of his, kissed it, and then closed his eyes.

"Saint was my big cousin. I loved 'em like a father," Drascilla said as she leveled the gun at Abrafo's head. She reached inside of her shirt, pulled out her thin gold necklace, and let it drop. The small crucifix snagged on the end of it, and it hung around her neck. "Like him, I'ma God-fearing person, so I'd like to recite something as I stand over you now..." She asked everyone present to close their eyes, bow their heads, and repeat after her. Once she'd seen they did, she said what she had in mind to say. "God, help Abrafo and his family discover your peace. Let them receive your comfort. Help them to be at rest knowing that you care for them, and that you love them. Calm their souls as they move into the afterlife. May they spend eternity with you. May they live forever in your presence. Amen."

Choot!

The bullet coming out of the silencer sounded like someone opening a soda can. Abrafo's head exploded upon impact, sending bloody chunks of meat and brain fragments flying in every direction. The blood poured out of the hole in his skull and expanded over the carpeted floor like a spilled can of paint.

"Drascilla," Patrick called for her attention. She turned around to him, and he was holding open a handkerchief. He nodded to the murder weapon in her hand, which told her he wanted it. Drascilla placed the gun in the handkerchief. He wiped the fingerprints from the blower, folded it up, and held it down at his side. "You guys go ahead and get outta here. My guys and I will see to it that this mess is cleaned up and these bodies are disposed of," he told Lachaun, Quan, Dr. CarMichael, and Drascilla.

"You sure? You know before I got saved I wasn't no stranger to this kinda work," Drascilla told him, with her hand on his shoulder.

"Yes, I'm sure, baby girl," Patrick replied, patting her hand with assurance.

"Okay. But you be sure to call me once you're home so I know you got in safely," Drascilla told him. Patrick nodded, and she kissed him on his cheek. Lachaun hugged and kissed him on the cheek before walking out of the office. Quan patted him on the shoulder and followed her out.

Dr. CarMichael walked up to Patrick, adjusting the jacket to his suit he'd draped over Dexter's dead body.

"I'm sorry this happened, Mr. Markham. Your son was a great man," Dr. CarMichael told him, placing his hand on his shoulder. "He meant a lot to me and a substantial amount of people. I just want chu to know that." He opened his arms for a hug.

"Thanks, son," Patrick replied and embraced him, patting his back.

"You got my line, so you call me if you need anything, OG," Dr. CarMichael told him with his hand on his shoulder. "And I do mean anything."

"I will," Patrick told him. "Be sure to lock that door on your way out."

"Sure thing," Dr. CarMichael said, patting him on his shoulder as he headed for the door. On his way out, the two Italian men were coming back inside of the office with big leather bags. The doctor was sure they had all kinds of shit in them that would help them chop up the bodies and clean up the bloody mess.

The Italian men took out hair caps, plastic face masks, gloves, shoe coverings, and surgical gowns from one of their leather bags. Once they'd gotten dressed, they withdrew shiny metal surgical tools from one bag to begin the process of cutting up the bodies. One of them pulled out a small radio, placed it on the desk top, and turned it on to Frank Sinatra's "The Best Is Yet to Come." A song they both loved. Patrick stood off to the side smoking a fat ass 5 Vegas cigar and watching the men work.

***

Assassin's downfall turned out to be a blessing in disguise for Vato. He and Shaniqua being out of the picture had left the community they had on lock wide open to solicitation for good dope. Vato saw the opportunity and jumped at the chance to seize it. It took some time, but he managed to link up with some out of town nigga from the windy city of Chicago. In exchange for him putting in a little grunt work for him, he hit him with a nice ticket price on some birds of raw. The product was decent enough for Vato to step on and make more profit. He even went so far as to label his dope 'Killuh,' like Hitt-Man and Assassin before him. That brand was established in the streets, and the dopeheads were fucking with it hard. So, he'd have to be a fool to run with a new name and have to build its reputation from scratch.

Vato saw great success in the dope game. He was getting more money than he knew what to do with and buying shit he couldn't even pronounce. He had designer clothes, luxury whips, jewels that rappers flaunted on television, two baby mansions, and a bad bitch for every day of the week. With his newfound wealth, the young nigga became arrogant and egotistical. He started thinking he was God's gift to the world and shit. What was even worse was he thought he could do whatever the fuck he wanted to do and get away with it because he was paid.

He made his mistake when he started beating on little mama that lived across the hall from him in his old apartment complex though. You see, that night, he went to the store to get whatever liquor she wanted to drink when they linked up, and his dog ass forgot to purchase the condoms along with it. He fucked around and got her pregnant that same night. Shorty winded up getting pregnant two more times by him on his way to dopeboy stardom. They were supposedly in a relationship, but he was always fucking around on her. On top of that, he was beating her ass over every little thing she did that irritated him. Buying her fancy things and taking her out to five-star restaurants was his way of apologizing. She'd eventually forgive him and things would go back to normal, as usual. But this last time, he went entirely too far.

Little mama had found out she was three months pregnant with their fourth child. When she broke the news to Vato, he wasn't the least bit happy. He tried to convince her to get an abortion, but that was out of the question. She reasoned that abortion was murder, and she wasn't going to sentence her child to death. Vato snapped and whipped her ass until she winded up losing the baby. Little mama ended up in the hospital, and when the police came around asking questions, she refused to give her baby daddy up. Although the cops couldn't get her to give up the name of the person who'd assaulted her, there was one man who managed to do what they couldn't, and that was her father— Narcotics Detective Gill Kramer.

Detective Kramer entered the baby mansion Vato shared with his daughter with a key she'd provided. He knocked him out cold while he was taking a piss, bound him to a chair with duct tape, and gagged his mouth. When the young nigga finally came around, Detective Kramer used a staple gun to pin his nutsack to his inner thigh and his dick to his stomach. He threatened to staple his eyelids shut if he didn't give him the combination to his safe. Vato gave him the combo, and he'd been gone for the past five minutes.

Vato sat in the center of the living room floor with his head bowed, wondering what the shady detective had in store for him. Hearing footfalls descending the staircase, he looked up to see Detective Kramer with a pillowcase slung over his shoulder. The pillowcase was lumpy with stacks of money he was positive came from his safe. His heart sank, knowing that all the loot he had in the world was now in the possession of his baby mama's father.

"Now, I didn't exactly count it, but I estimate you've got at least 350 Gs here. And that's just a wild guess. I could be wrong," Detective Kramer said as he reached the landing, taking a swig from his flask. He dropped the pillowcase at his feet, screwed the cap back on his flask, and secured it back inside of his suit's jacket. "This right here is more than enough for me to pay off my bookie as well as pay off a couple of bills. The rest I'ma kick up to Stephanie and my grandbabies." He started whistling as he pulled a black pistol from the small of his back with his black leather-gloved hand and screwed a silencer on its barrel. As soon as Vato saw the gun, his eyes got big and his heart thudded mercilessly.

"The day you raised yo' fucking hand to my daughter was the day you sentenced yourself to death, you lil' shit," Detective

Kramer snarled as he aimed the pistol at Vato. The young nigga thrashed around, trying to break free of his bondages, to no avail. It was all over for him!

Choot!

The bullet zipped across the living room, went through Vato's left eye, and left a huge hole in the back of his skull. His blood misted the air, and his head dropped to his chest. Droplets of blood dripped from the hole in his forehead and splashed on the floor between his feet.

Detective Kramer lowered the pistol and took a prolonged look at his kill. He tossed the murder weapon at Vato's feet, hoisted the pillowcase over his shoulder, and headed towards the front door. He pulled out his cellphone and hit up his bookie.

"Aye, Sal, I've got that paypa you've been breathing down my neck about," Detective Kramer said into his cellular. "No, I didn't rob a bank. What do you take me for, a criminal? Hahaha, very funny. Listen, I'd like to drop twenty grand on the Raiders game. How's six points?"

***

Quan walked down the stairs in her robe and a pair of fluffy, wool house slippers. Every now and again, she dabbed her eyes with a balled-up Kleenex. Her eyes were pink and had bags below them from crying for hours. She couldn't help the feeling that Zekey was dead. For some odd reason, she kept seeing his lifeless face flash before her eyes. The thought of him never coming back to her hurt like hell, and crippled her emotionally and physically. He was her soul mate, her better half, her everything, and she didn't know how she'd go on living without him.

Ali had been out for days, scouring the streets for Zekey. Unfortunately, he couldn't find him or anyone with information on the ho-ass niggaz that kidnapped him. When he'd come home, she could see the pain and defeated look in his eyes. She comforted him and made him his favorite meal, but he didn't take any more than a couple of bites before excusing himself from the table. This saddened her, but she knew there wasn't anything she could do to make him feel better. She was convinced that he'd only feel better if Zekey returned home, but two days with him having been missing, she knew that the chances of that were highly unlikely.

Ali had gone upstairs to his bedroom. Quan could smell the unmistakable odor of weed seeping from underneath his door, but she decided to leave him to his vice. She normally didn't allow him to get high in the house, but she understood that putting one in the air was his way of coping with the kidnapping of his stepfather.

Quan sat down on the couch before a bottle of red wine and a glass she'd left on the coffee table before she'd put EJ to bed. She poured herself a half glass of wine, scooped up the glass, and picked up the remote control. She turned on the flat-screen television set and flipped through the channels. Finding an interesting movie on the Lifetime channel, she sat the remote control beside her and focused her attention on the screen. She was about to take another sip of her alcoholic beverage when she suddenly gotten a whiff of a very pleasant smell. She held her glass at her lips as her forehead wrinkled and her nose twitched.

Quan sat the wine glass down on the coffee table and looked around the living room. What she'd smelled was Zekey's favorite cologne, Armani Code. She'd gotten it for him on the first day he'd come home from prison.

"Baby, is that you? Are you home?" Quan asked and sprang to her feat. She ran around the house looking in every room on the ground level. When she didn't see him, she hurried up the stairs, tripping and falling along the way. She got back up on her feet, limping up the rest of the steps having sprung her ankle. "Zekey? Baby? Are you home?"

Quan ran back and forth across the upstairs looking for Zekey. When she didn't see him, she rapped on Ali's door frantically. As soon as Ali opened the door, she was smacked in the face with the smell of weed and lavender Glad air freshener. Ali's eyes were glassy and red webbed, so she could tell he was as high as the moon.

"What's up, Mom?" Ali asked as he yanked the Beats by Dre headphones from his ears.

"Is Zekey up in here?" Quan asked. Before he could answer, she burst into his bedroom and searched high and low for her husband. She then raced out of the bedroom and down the stairs with Ali following behind her.

"Ma, what makes you think Pops is here? You seen 'em?" Ali asked with lines across his forehead. He was confused and didn't know what was going on.

"No, I—I—I smelled 'em, well, I smell his cologne!" Quan darted to the front door, unchaining and unlocking it. She snatched it open and looked around outside. Zekey wasn't anywhere in sight. She sighed sadly, and her shoulders slumped. Tears danced in her eyes, and her bottom lip shivered. She was terribly hurt and dreading the day she'd get a phone call for her to come identify a body that may be her husband's.

Disappointed, Quan shut and locked the front door. When she turned around, Ali could see the hurt in her eyes, and he felt sorry for her. He knew how much his mother loved Zekey, and he could only imagine how she was feeling with his kidnapping. Quan's eyes overflowed with tears, and her shoulders rocked. She broke down sobbing, with snot threatening to drip from her left nostril.

"Awww, Ma, come here," Ali said and opened his arms to her. Head bowed, Quan walked into her son's arms, and he wrapped them around her. He kissed her on top of her head and rubbed her back. "It's gonna be okay, Ma, you'll see. We haven't heard the last of 'em yet," he assured her as she wept in his arms.

"Quan—Ali—Quan—Ali—" The characters from various TV shows and movies echoed their names as the channels changed on their own.

Quan and Ali exchanged frowns then looked at the flat-screen television. Ali led his mother by the hand over to the couch, and they sat down.

"Zekey, is—is that you?" Quan asked, staring at the television's screen.

"Yes—it's—me—" The channels changed using different characters from shows and movies to answer her question.

"Yo, this shit crazy!" Ali said, wide eyed with disbelief dripping from his every word. "Yo, Pops, it's me—Ali. Are you alive?"

When Ali asked this, the TV was allowing an episode of *Two and a Half Men* to play. Then, suddenly, the channel changed again.

"No!"

"Oh, my god!" Quan shouted and burst into tears again. She slapped her hands over her nose and mouth. Again, her shoulders rocked as she sobbed loudly. Ali, who was silently crying, wrapped his arms around her to console her.

"I—have—to—go now—but—always remember—I love you—" The channels changed, making another statement. "Quan—Ali—and—E—J."

Quan sobbed louder and louder, hearing Zekey's last words. Ali held her tighter and rubbed her back to sooth her suffering. The tears continued to flow out of their eyes, and they didn't show any signs of stopping.

***

"That's a very interesting story. So, you're the last of the OGs?" Kevin asked OG while sitting at his bedside holding a mop handle in his tattooed hands. He'd been listening intently to the story he'd been told. Kevin was a stocky, muscular young man with frizzy cornrows. The back of his neck was inked with the neighborhood he'd pledged allegiance to at eleven years old. He wore a white thermal shirt underneath a navy-blue, short-sleeve Dickie jumpsuit with his work I.D. badge hanging from his breast pocket.

"Y—yeah, the last of 'em—le—left. I'm the last—I'm the last of the OGs," OG said as he lay up in bed with a see-through nasal cannula in his nostrils, which helped him breathed. Lung cancer had taken a serious toll on his physical appearance. His skin had darkened, and he'd lost an incredible amount of weight, seventy-five pounds to be exact. The skeletal bone structure of his face, chest, and arms shone. The old man looked like an unwrapped mummy. His head and face were covered in white stubble from his hair beginning to grow back. His eyes were sunken into their sockets, and there were black bags under them.

Under a new state law that made chronically as well as terminally ill inmates eligible for early release, OG was released to a hospice home. Thanks to Lachaun, he was afforded the best care money could buy. And since the hospice home wasn't too far from her mansion, she and Billion would come to visit him every day.

Kevin glanced at his black digital timepiece, and his eyebrows rose with surprise. He got up from the chair and placed it back where he'd gotten it from. He then stuck the mop back inside of its yellow push bucket and approached OG's bedside. The two of them had formed quite the bond since the old man's arrival. They'd taken a liking to each other. Kevin would go out his way to drop by his room and holla at him. Sometimes, he'd spend his entire lunch break up in OG's room, eating and listening to his throwback gangsta stories. Old head could tell one hell of a story. He could sit there and listen to him for hours.

"Aye, Pops," Kevin began, resting his hand on his arm. "I gotta get back to work, but chu take it easy. I'ma drop by and holla at chu once I'm off the clock. Okay?"

"Unh, huh," OG replied weakly with hooded eyes.

"Alright then, man, stay strong," Kevin told him. He then looked over his room at all of the colorful balloons, flowers, and cards his family had brought him. There were even pictures Billion had drawn tacked to the wall above the old man's bed. Kevin smiled, thinking about how loved OG was by his relatives. He knew then his passing was going to hurt his family tremendously. Although he hated the thought of him dying, it was inevitable, and there wasn't anything he could do about it.

"I'm the last—I'm the last of the OGs—" OG recited over and over again, his voice getting fainter and fainter, his eyes closing further and further.

Kevin made his way down the hallway, pushing the yellow mop bucket with the mop handle. Along the way, he saw Lachaun and nine-year-old Billion at the check-in station. He always seemed to run into them whenever he was coming to OG's room or leaving it. Today wasn't any different from any other.

"What up, y'all?" Kevin greeted them with a smile.

"What's up, Kev?" Billion replied with a grin and dapped him up. Lachaun had smoothed the sticky visitor's pass over the right side of her shirt and had started to smooth Billion's sticky pass over his shirt.

"Ain't nothing, lil' homie," Kevin replied.

"Hey, Kev," Lachaun greeted him with a smile and gave him a hug.

"'Sup, Mrs. James?" Kevin replied, hugging her back. "Man, you smell hella good. What chu got on?" he asked as they broke their embrace, holding on to her waist a little longer than he should have. As quiet as it was kept, though she was half his age, he had a thing for her. Lachaun knew he did too, but she wasn't ready to start back dating after losing her husband. She was still trying to give her heart some time to heal.

"Jimmy Choo Signature. You like?" Lachaun asked, smiling and sweeping her micro individual braids over her shoulder.

"Like?" He leaned toward her neck, closed his eyes, and inhaled the lovely fragrance. "I love it."

"Well, thank you." Lachaun blushed with a smile.

"You're welcome, Mrs. James," Kevin said.

"Oh, please, call me Lachaun or Chaun," she replied, smiling harder. Billion looked back and forth between his mother and Kevin. He could tell his mother was smitten with Kevin, and he didn't mind if she decided to date him. It had been a year since his father had been murdered, and he felt it was time she moved on.

"I'm sorry, Chaun," Kevin said, looking at her sexily and licking his lips. The way he was looking at her made her heart flutter. She thought Kevin was hood and fine as fuck. He really turned her on. "I gotta get going, so I'll holla at y'all later."

"Okay, see you later," Lachaun told him with a short wave. She watched as he and Billion threw playful punches at each other.

"I see you been working on that jab, big dog," Kevin said with a smile. He ruffled Billion's head and walked away, pushing the yellow mop bucket.

Lachaun and Billion walked down the hallway toward OG's room.

"Momma, look at chu cheesing. You like Kev, huh?" Billion asked.

Lachaun blushed and chuckled. "Now, what gave you that idea?"

Billion mocked his mother's interaction with Kevin, "Oh, please, call me Lachaun or Chaun."

Lachaun threw her head back, laughing, and playfully shoved her son. "Boy, shut up, I did not say it like that."

"Unh, huh. Yes, you did." Billion smiled.

"Whatever." Lachaun grinned and pulled him closer, kissing the top of his head. They continued down the corridor toward OG's room.

***

"I'm the last—The Last of the OGs—Haaaa." OG took his last breath. His chest rose and fell for the last time, and his muscles relaxed. He lay there with his eyes closed and his mouth stuck open. The green zig zag line of the heart monitor went up one last time with a beep, then the zig zag line went completely flat. Then, there was an annoying prolonged beeping. It resonated inside of his room and spilled outside into the hallway.

Lachaun and Billion raced down the hallway and bent the corner inside of OG's room. Their eyes exploded open in fear, and their hearts sank to the pit of their stomachs when they saw OG lying still in bed.

"Oh my god, no! No!" Lachaun screamed and shouted with tears flooding her cheeks. She ran over to OG's bedside and shook him gently at first and then harder.

"Grandpa James! Grandpa James, please don't die!" Billion sobbed loudly with a tear-soaked face while holding his grandfather's hand. The teardrops dripped from his eyes, splashing on his sneakers and the floor. "Don't leave us, we need you." Billion, still holding his grandfather's hand, bowed his head to his hand and dropped down to his knees. His shoulders quaked as he whimpered long and loud.

Lachaun laid her head against his chest and sobbed just as loudly as Billion. The tears seemed to pour down her cheeks in buckets.

The nursing home staff was running as fast as they could to get to OG's room. One of them was pushing a cart with a defibrillator on top of it. They spilled inside of the room and pulled Lachaun and Billion away from OG's bedside. They quickly removed his powder blue hospital gown, lubed up the defibrillator cups, and pressed them onto his bony chest. The cups sent an electrical charge into OG's heart, and his body jerked violently. They tried over and over again, but unfortunately, their efforts were to no avail.

The Last of the OGs was dead!

THE END

Submission Guideline

Submit the first three chapters of your completed manuscript to
ldpsubmissions@gmail.com, subject line: Your book's title. The
manuscript must be in a .doc file and sent as an attachment.
Document should be in Times New Roman, double spaced and in
size 12 font. Also, provide your synopsis and full contact information. If sending multiple submissions, they must each be in a
separate email.

Have a story but no way to send it electronically? You can still
submit to LDP/Ca$h Presents. Send in the first three chapters,
written or typed, of your completed manuscript to:

LDP: Submissions Dept
Po Box 944
Stockbridge, Ga 30281

DO NOT send original manuscript. Must be a duplicate.

Provide your synopsis and a cover letter containing your full
contact information.

Thanks for considering LDP and Ca$h Presents.

The Last of the OGs 3

Coming Soon from Lock Down Publications/Ca$h Presents

BOW DOWN TO MY GANGSTA

By **Ca$h**

TORN BETWEEN TWO

By **Coffee**

BLOOD OF A BOSS **VI**

SHADOWS OF THE GAME II

TRAP BASTARD II

By **Askari**

LOYAL TO THE GAME **IV**

By **T.J. & Jelissa**

IF LOVING YOU IS WRONG… **III**

By **Jelissa**

TRUE SAVAGE **VIII**

MIDNIGHT CARTEL IV

DOPE BOY MAGIC IV

CITY OF KINGZ III

By **Chris Green**

BLAST FOR ME **III**

A SAVAGE DOPEBOY III

CUTTHROAT MAFIA III

DUFFLE BAG CARTEL VII

HEARTLESS GOON VI

By **Ghost**

A HUSTLER'S DECEIT III

KILL ZONE **II**

BAE BELONGS TO ME III

A DOPE BOY'S QUEEN III

By **Aryanna**

Tranay Adams

COKE KINGS V

KING OF THE TRAP III

By **T.J. Edwards**

GORILLAZ IN THE BAY V

3X KRAZY III

De'Kari

THE STREETS ARE CALLING II

Duquie Wilson

KINGPIN KILLAZ IV

STREET KINGS III

PAID IN BLOOD III

CARTEL KILLAZ IV

DOPE GODS III

Hood Rich

SINS OF A HUSTLA II

ASAD

KINGZ OF THE GAME VI

Playa Ray

SLAUGHTER GANG IV

RUTHLESS HEART IV

By Willie Slaughter

FUK SHYT II

By Blakk Diamond

TRAP QUEEN

RICH $AVAGE II

MONEY IN THE GRAVE II

By Troublesome

YAYO V

GHOST MOB II

Stilloan Robinson

CREAM III

By Yolanda Moore

SON OF A DOPE FIEND III

HEAVEN GOT A GHETTO II

By Renta

FOREVER GANGSTA II

GLOCKS ON SATIN SHEETS III

By Adrian Dulan

LOYALTY AIN'T PROMISED III

By Keith Williams

THE PRICE YOU PAY FOR LOVE III

By Destiny Skai

I'M NOTHING WITHOUT HIS LOVE II

SINS OF A THUG II

TO THE THUG I LOVED BEFORE II

By Monet Dragun

LIFE OF A SAVAGE IV

MURDA SEASON IV

GANGLAND CARTEL IV

CHI'RAQ GANGSTAS IV

KILLERS ON ELM STREET IV

JACK BOYZ N DA BRONX III

A DOPEBOY'S DREAM II

By **Romell Tukes**

QUIET MONEY IV

EXTENDED CLIP III

THUG LIFE IV

By **Trai'Quan**

THE STREETS MADE ME III

By **Larry D. Wright**

IF YOU CROSS ME ONCE II

ANGEL III

By **Anthony Fields**

FRIEND OR FOE III

By **Mimi**

SAVAGE STORMS III

By **Meesha**

THE STREETS WILL NEVER CLOSE II

By K'ajji

IN THE ARM OF HIS BOSS

By Jamila

HARD AND RUTHLESS III

MOB TOWN 251 II

By Von Diesel

LEVELS TO THIS SHYT II

By Ah'Million

MOB TIES III

By SayNoMore

FOR THE LOVE OF A BOSS III

By C. D. Blue

MOBBED UP II

By King Rio

BRED IN THE GAME II

By S. Allen

KILLA KOUNTY II

By Khufu

The Last of the OGs 3

Available Now

RESTRAINING ORDER **I & II**

By **CA$H & Coffee**

LOVE KNOWS NO BOUNDARIES **I II & III**

By **Coffee**

RAISED AS A GOON I, II, III & IV

BRED BY THE SLUMS I, II, III

BLAST FOR ME I & II

ROTTEN TO THE CORE I II III

A BRONX TALE I, II, III

DUFFLE BAG CARTEL I II III IV V VI

HEARTLESS GOON I II III IV V

A SAVAGE DOPEBOY I II

DRUG LORDS I II III

CUTTHROAT MAFIA I II

By **Ghost**

LAY IT DOWN **I & II**

LAST OF A DYING BREED I II

BLOOD STAINS OF A SHOTTA I & II III

By **Jamaica**

LOYAL TO THE GAME I II III

LIFE OF SIN I, II III

By **TJ & Jelissa**

BLOODY COMMAS I & II

SKI MASK CARTEL I II & III

KING OF NEW YORK I II,III IV V

RISE TO POWER I II III

COKE KINGS I II III IV

191

Tranay Adams

BORN HEARTLESS I II III IV

KING OF THE TRAP I II

By **T.J. Edwards**

IF LOVING HIM IS WRONG…I & II

LOVE ME EVEN WHEN IT HURTS I II III

By **Jelissa**

WHEN THE STREETS CLAP BACK I & II III

THE HEART OF A SAVAGE I II III

By **Jibril Williams**

A DISTINGUISHED THUG STOLE MY HEART I II & III

LOVE SHOULDN'T HURT I II III IV

RENEGADE BOYS I II III IV

PAID IN KARMA I II III

SAVAGE STORMS I II

AN UNFORESEEN LOVE

By **Meesha**

A GANGSTER'S CODE I &, II III

A GANGSTER'S SYN I II III

THE SAVAGE LIFE I II III

CHAINED TO THE STREETS I II III

BLOOD ON THE MONEY I II III

By J-Blunt

PUSH IT TO THE LIMIT

By **Bre' Hayes**

BLOOD OF A BOSS **I, II, III, IV, V**

SHADOWS OF THE GAME

TRAP BASTARD

By **Askari**

THE STREETS BLEED MURDER **I, II & III**

THE HEART OF A GANGSTA I II& III

192

The Last of the OGs 3

By **Jerry Jackson**
CUM FOR ME I II III IV V VI VII
An **LDP Erotica Collaboration**
BRIDE OF A HUSTLA **I II & II**
THE FETTI GIRLS **I, II& III**
CORRUPTED BY A GANGSTA I, II III, IV
BLINDED BY HIS LOVE
THE PRICE YOU PAY FOR LOVE I II
DOPE GIRL MAGIC I II III
By **Destiny Skai**
WHEN A GOOD GIRL GOES BAD
By **Adrienne**
THE COST OF LOYALTY I II III
By Kweli
A GANGSTER'S REVENGE **I II III & IV**
THE BOSS MAN'S DAUGHTERS I II III IV V
A SAVAGE LOVE **I & II**
BAE BELONGS TO ME I II
A HUSTLER'S DECEIT I, II, III
WHAT BAD BITCHES DO I, II, III
SOUL OF A MONSTER I II III
KILL ZONE
A DOPE BOY'S QUEEN I II
By **Aryanna**
A KINGPIN'S AMBITON
A KINGPIN'S AMBITION **II**
I MURDER FOR THE DOUGH
By **Ambitious**
TRUE SAVAGE I II III IV V VI VII
DOPE BOY MAGIC I, II, III

Tranay Adams

MIDNIGHT CARTEL I II III

CITY OF KINGZ I II

By **Chris Green**

A DOPEBOY'S PRAYER

By **Eddie "Wolf" Lee**

THE KING CARTEL **I, II & III**

By **Frank Gresham**

THESE NIGGAS AIN'T LOYAL **I, II & III**

By **Nikki Tee**

GANGSTA SHYT **I II &III**

By **CATO**

THE ULTIMATE BETRAYAL

By **Phoenix**

BOSS'N UP **I , II & III**

By **Royal Nicole**

I LOVE YOU TO DEATH

By Destiny J

I RIDE FOR MY HITTA

I STILL RIDE FOR MY HITTA

By **Misty Holt**

LOVE & CHASIN' PAPER

By **Qay Crockett**

TO DIE IN VAIN

SINS OF A HUSTLA

By **ASAD**

BROOKLYN HUSTLAZ

By **Boogsy Morina**

BROOKLYN ON LOCK I & II

By **Sonovia**

GANGSTA CITY

The Last of the OGs 3

By **Teddy Duke**

A DRUG KING AND HIS DIAMOND I & II III

A DOPEMAN'S RICHES

HER MAN, MINE'S TOO I, II

CASH MONEY HO'S

THE WIFEY I USED TO BE I II

By Nicole Goosby

TRAPHOUSE KING **I II & III**

KINGPIN KILLAZ I II III

STREET KINGS I II

PAID IN BLOOD **I II**

CARTEL KILLAZ I II III

DOPE GODS I II

By **Hood Rich**

LIPSTICK KILLAH **I, II, III**

CRIME OF PASSION I II & III

FRIEND OR FOE I II

By **Mimi**

STEADY MOBBN' **I, II, III**

THE STREETS STAINED MY SOUL I II

By **Marcellus Allen**

WHO SHOT YA **I, II, III**

SON OF A DOPE FIEND I II

HEAVEN GOT A GHETTO

Renta

GORILLAZ IN THE BAY **I II III IV**

TEARS OF A GANGSTA I II

3X KRAZY I II

DE'KARI

TRIGGADALE I II III

Tranay Adams

Elijah R. Freeman

GOD BLESS THE TRAPPERS I, II, III

THESE SCANDALOUS STREETS I, II, III

FEAR MY GANGSTA I, II, III IV, V

THESE STREETS DON'T LOVE NOBODY I, II

BURY ME A G I, II, III, IV, V

A GANGSTA'S EMPIRE I, II, III, IV

THE DOPEMAN'S BODYGAURD I II

THE REALEST KILLAZ I II III

THE LAST OF THE OGS I II III

Tranay Adams

THE STREETS ARE CALLING

Duquie Wilson

MARRIED TO A BOSS... I II III

By Destiny Skai & Chris Green

KINGZ OF THE GAME I II III IV V

Playa Ray

SLAUGHTER GANG I II III

RUTHLESS HEART I II III

By Willie Slaughter

FUK SHYT

By Blakk Diamond

DON'T F#CK WITH MY HEART I II

By Linnea

ADDICTED TO THE DRAMA I II III

IN THE ARM OF HIS BOSS II

By Jamila

YAYO I II III IV

A SHOOTER'S AMBITION I II

BRED IN THE GAME

The Last of the OGs 3

By S. Allen
TRAP GOD I II III
RICH $AVAGE
MONEY IN THE GRAVE
By Troublesome
FOREVER GANGSTA
GLOCKS ON SATIN SHEETS I II
By Adrian Dulan
TOE TAGZ I II III
LEVELS TO THIS SHYT
By Ah'Million
KINGPIN DREAMS I II III
By Paper Boi Rari
CONFESSIONS OF A GANGSTA I II III
By Nicholas Lock
I'M NOTHING WITHOUT HIS LOVE
SINS OF A THUG
TO THE THUG I LOVED BEFORE
By Monet Dragun
CAUGHT UP IN THE LIFE I II III
By Robert Baptiste
NEW TO THE GAME I II III
MONEY, MURDER & MEMORIES I II III
By **Malik D. Rice**
LIFE OF A SAVAGE I II III
A GANGSTA'S QUR'AN I II III
MURDA SEASON I II III
GANGLAND CARTEL I II III
CHI'RAQ GANGSTAS I II III

Tranay Adams

KILLERS ON ELM STREET I II III

JACK BOYZ N DA BRONX I II

A DOPEBOY'S DREAM

By **Romell Tukes**

LOYALTY AIN'T PROMISED I II

By Keith Williams

QUIET MONEY I II III

THUG LIFE I II III

EXTENDED CLIP I II

By **Trai'Quan**

THE STREETS MADE ME I II

By **Larry D. Wright**

THE ULTIMATE SACRIFICE I, II, III, IV, V, VI

KHADIFI

IF YOU CROSS ME ONCE

ANGEL I II

IN THE BLINK OF AN EYE

By **Anthony Fields**

THE LIFE OF A HOOD STAR

By Ca$h & Rashia Wilson

THE STREETS WILL NEVER CLOSE

By K'ajji

CREAM I II

By Yolanda Moore

NIGHTMARES OF A HUSTLA I II III

By King Dream

CONCRETE KILLA I II

By Kingpen

HARD AND RUTHLESS I II

MOB TOWN 251

The Last of the OGs 3

By Von Diesel

GHOST MOB II

Stilloan Robinson

MOB TIES I II

By SayNoMore

BODYMORE MURDERLAND I II III

By Delmont Player

FOR THE LOVE OF A BOSS I II

By C. D. Blue

MOBBED UP

By King Rio

KILLA KOUNTY

By Khufu

Tranay Adams

BOOKS BY LDP'S CEO, CA$H

TRUST IN NO MAN

TRUST IN NO MAN 2

TRUST IN NO MAN 3

BONDED BY BLOOD

SHORTY GOT A THUG

THUGS CRY

THUGS CRY 2

THUGS CRY 3

TRUST NO BITCH

TRUST NO BITCH 2

TRUST NO BITCH 3

TIL MY CASKET DROPS

RESTRAINING ORDER

RESTRAINING ORDER 2

IN LOVE WITH A CONVICT

LIFE OF A HOOD STAR

The Last of the OGs 3

CPSIA information can be obtained
at www.ICGtesting.com
Printed in the USA
LVHW051756191121
703844LV00017B/1461